CREATURES OF THE COSMOS

Creatures of the Cosmos

CATHERINE CROOK DE CAMP
Editor

Illustrated by
JAY KRUSH

THE WESTMINSTER PRESS
Philadelphia

Book Design by Dorothy Alden Smith

Published by The Westminster Press®
Philadelphia, Pennsylvania

PRINTED IN THE UNITED STATES OF AMERICA

9 8 7 6 5 4 3 2 1

"The Bear Who Saved the World," based on "The Command," by L.
Sprague de Camp, from *Astounding Science Fiction,* October 1938.
Copyright © 1938, Street & Smith Publications, Inc.; renewed 1966, L.
Sprague de Camp.

"Old Man Henderson," by Kris Neville, from *Fantasy and Science Fiction,*
June 1951. Copyright © 1951, Fantasy House, Inc. Reprinted by permission of Forrest J. Ackerman, Agent.

"The Smallest Dragonboy," by Anne McCaffrey. Copyright © 1974, Anne
McCaffrey. Repr. by permission of author and Virginia Kidd, Agent.

"The Large Ant," by Howard Fast, published as "The Big Ant," in *Fantastic Universe.* Copyright © 1960, Great American Publications, Inc.
Copyright assigned 1960 to Howard Fast. Repr. by permission of author.

"Dead Man's Chest," by L. Sprague de Camp, from *The Magazine of
Fantasy and Science Fiction.* Copyright © 1977, Mercury Press, Inc.
Reprinted by permission of the author.

"Socrates," by John Christopher, from *Galaxy Magazine,* March 1951.
Copyright © 1951, Galaxy Publishing Corporation. Reprinted by permission of the author.

Library of Congress Cataloging in Publication Data

    Main entry under title:
Creatures of the cosmos.
  Bibliography: p.
  CONTENTS: De Camp, L. S. and De Camp, C. C. The bear
who saved the world.—Neville, K. Old Man Henderson.—
De Camp, C. C. The million dollar pup. [etc.]
    1. Science fiction, American. 2. Animals, Legends and
stories of. 1. Science fiction. 2. Animals—Fiction.
3. Short stories I. De Camp, Catherine Crook.
II. Krush, Jay
PZ5.C892   [Fic]   77–22748
ISBN 0–664–32621–8

*To readers of all ages
who love creatures,
great or small*

Contents

Continued

A Word from the Editor

Here are eight tales about beasts that never were, on land, on sea, or in the air.

One of these creatures of the cosmos was brought to Earth from Venus. Two others came from planets that circle distant stars. One Earth animal thinks like a human being because a scientist operated on his brain. Another not only thinks, but also talks, because he is a mutant, a living thing whose heredity was made over by atomic radiation.

Two creatures have ESP (extrasensory perception), the ability to read another person's mind and send thought messages. One creature is a cynoid, a remarkable creation. Another is a unique and terrifying ancient sea monster. Have fun reading about them!

9

1

The Bear
Who Saved the World

by
L. Sprague and Catherine Crook de Camp

Johnny Black pulled Volume 5 of the *Britannica* off the
library shelf and opened it to the article on "Chemistry." Adjusting the elastic that held his spectacles in
place, he worried his way through a few paragraphs
before he decided, sadly, that he could go no farther
until his man, Professor Mettin, explained things to
him. And he wanted so much to learn all about chemistry and the chemicals that had made it possible for him
to read at all!

Johnny Black was not human, and he knew it. He
was, instead, a fine specimen of the American black
bear, *Euarctos americanus,* upon whose brain Professor
Mettin, chief of staff at the North American Biological
Research Station, had performed a remarkable experiment. Mettin had injected a chemical compound that
lowered the resistance of the synapses between the
cells of his small bear's brain so that the complicated
electrical process called thought became as easy for
Johnny as for a man.

The bear continued to turn the pages of the encyclo-
pedia carefully with his paw. He had once tried using

12

his tongue, but the sharp edges of the paper had cut it. Besides, his master had scolded him for dampening the pages of a valuable book. After Johnny had read the article on "Chess," he stowed his spectacles in the case attached to his collar and ambled outdoors.

The island of St. Croix sweltered under a Caribbean sun. The blue of the sky and the green of the hills were lost on Johnny, who, like all bears, was color-blind. He regretted that his bear's eyesight was not keen enough to make out the boats in Frederiksted harbor. His poor eyesight together with a lack of fingers to manipulate things and lack of vocal organs adapted to speech were Johnny's chief grievances. He sometimes wished that if he had to be an animal with a human brain, he were an ape like McGinty, the chimpanzee.

Johnny began to wonder about McGinty. He hadn't heard a peep out of him all morning, whereas the old ape usually shrieked and threw things at everybody who went by. Curious, Johnny shuffled over to the cages. The monkeys chattered at him as usual, but the ape sat with his back to the wall, staring blankly. When Johnny growled a little, McGinty's eyes swung at the sound, his limbs stirred, but he did not get up. He must be pretty sick, thought Johnny, then comforted himself with the fact that within the hour Pablo would be around to feed the animals and would report McGinty's strange behavior to Professor Mettin.

Thinking about food reminded Johnny that it was high time for Honoria, the cook, to ring the Station bell that summoned the scientists to lunch. But no bell rang. In fact, the place seemed unnaturally quiet. Besides the chirping of the birds and the chattering of the monkeys, the only sound he heard was the *put-put-put* of a stationary engine at Bemis' place, beyond the grounds of the Biological Research Station.

13

Bemis was a botanist who had recently received a U.S. Government grant to set up a laboratory on St. Croix. He had settled in on a property next to the Research Station. Johnny knew that the scientists at the Research Station did not like Bemis. They called him "eccentric" and wondered about the little plump man who swaggered around in riding boots when there wasn't a horse in the area. Johnny wanted to investigate the stationary engine, but he remembered the fuss Bemis had made the last time he had wandered over.

He decided instead to investigate the delayed luncheon. Trotting over to the Station kitchen, he put his muzzle in the door. He did not go farther, remembering the cook's unreasonable attitude toward bears in her kitchen. He smelled burning food and saw Honoria, mountainous as ever, sitting by the window looking at nothing.

Alarmed, Johnny set out to find Mettin. Although the professor was not in the social room, the rest of the staff were gathered there. Dr. Breuker, an authority on the psychology of speech, sat in an easy chair, a newspaper across his lap. He didn't move when Johnny sniffed his leg. He had dropped a lighted cigarette on the rug, where it had burned a large hole before going out. Doctors Markel and Ryerson and Ryerson's wife were there too, sitting like so many statues.

Eventually, Johnny found the lanky Mettin, clad in underwear, lying on his bed, staring at the ceiling. He did not look sick, but he didn't move unless prodded or nipped. An hour later, Johnny gave up trying to get a sensible reaction out of any of the people at the Station. He went outside to think. He would call a physician if only he could speak. He might go down to Frederiksted to try to get one, but he would likely get shot for his pains.

14

Happening to glance toward Bemis' laboratory, Johnny was surprised to see something round rise into the sky, slowly dwindle, and vanish. He guessed that this was a small balloon, for he had heard that Bemis was planning a botanical experiment involving the use of balloons. Another sphere followed the first, then another, until they formed a continuous procession dwindling into nothingness.

This was too much for the curious bear. He had to find out why anyone would want to fill the heavens with balloons a yard in diameter. Besides, he hoped that Bemis might come over to the Station and see about the entranced staff.

Approaching the Bemis house, he saw a truck, a lot of machinery, a pile of unfilled balloons, and two unfamiliar men. The men inflated the balloons, one by one, attached a small box to each, and released them into the air.

One man caught sight of Johnny, yelled, "Hey!" and reached for his holster. Although Johnny rose on his hind legs and gravely extended his right paw in greeting, the man shouted, "Get out of here, you!"

When Johnny, puzzled, hesitated, the man jerked out his pistol and fired. Johnny felt a stunning blow as the .38 slug glanced off his thick skull. The next instant, gravel flying, he streaked for the Station.

Back home, he found a bathroom mirror and inspected the gash on his forehead. Since he could not apply a bandage, he ran cold water over the wound until the bleeding stopped. Weak with hunger, he made his way to the kitchen. There he used his claws as natural can openers and poured a can of peaches down his throat. A moment later, he heard a truck back up to the kitchen door. He slipped noiselessly into the dining room.

The kitchen door slammed. The raw voice of the man who had shot at him spoke to Honoria, "What's your name, huh?"

Toneless, the woman replied, "Honoria Velez."

"Okay, Honoria, you help us carry this food out to the truck." Johnny could hear the slapping of Honoria's slippers as she moved about, arms full of provisions, docilely piling cans into the truck. When the men said, "That's all," she sat down on the kitchen steps, dazed and unmoving. The truck drove off.

It had occurred to Johnny, as he watched through the crack of the dining room door, that these men, their balloons, and the trancelike state of the people at the Station were somehow related. More curious than ever, he hurried out and headed for a clump of trees standing on a rise at the end of the Station property.

From this hidden observation post, he watched as more and more balloons sailed off into the sky. Eventually, the two men at work were joined by two others from the bungalow. The stocky figure, Johnny decided, was Bemis. If that were so, the botanist must be the mastermind of the gang of swaggering ruffians. And he, Johnny, had at least four enemies to deal with. How, he didn't know.

First, he considered Honoria's actions. The cook, normally a strong-minded person of granite stubbornness, had carried out every order without a peep. Yet Honoria had remembered her name and understood orders well enough. Evidently, the disease—or whatever it was—seemed not to affect the victim mentally or physically except to deprive him of initiative and willpower. Johnny wondered why he had not been affected also. Then, remembering the chimpanzee and the monkeys, he concluded that the disease was specific to the higher anthropoids.

16

Night descended, but in his hideaway Johnny had difficulty sleeping. Plans for attacking the bungalow swarmed like bees through his mind. He knew a night raid would be impossible because his eyesight was especially poor at night and because all four of his enemies would be together through the dark hours.

At sunrise, Johnny saw the two tough fellows start up the little engine and begin to inflate more balloons. Making a long detour, he sneaked up to the bungalow from the far side and crawled under the house. Like most houses in the Virgin Islands, the building had no cellar. He crept around softly until the scrape of feet on the thin floor above told him he was directly under the men within. Bemis was talking.

"... and those fools are caught in Havana with no way of getting down here, because transportation all over the Caribbean is tied up by now."

A British voice answered, "I suppose that in time it will occur to them to go to the owner of a boat or plane and simply tell the chap to bring them here. That's the only thing for them to do with everybody in Cuba under the influence of the molds by now, what? How many more balloons should we send up?"

"All we have," replied Bemis.

"But, I say, oughtn't we keep some in reserve? It wouldn't do to have to spend the rest of our lives sending spores up into the stratosphere, in the hope that the cosmic rays will give us another mutation like this one."

"I said we'll send up all the *balloons*, not all the *spores*, Forney. I have plenty of those in reserve, and I'm growing more from my molds all the time. Anyway, suppose we did run out of molds before all the world is infected—which it will be in a few weeks. There wasn't one chance in a million of that first mutation, yet it happened. That's how I know it was a sign from above.

I have been chosen to lead the world out of its errors and confusions, and I shall do it. The Lord gave me this power over the world, and He shall not fail me!"

So, thought Johnny, that was it. He knew that Bemis was an expert on molds. The botanist must have sent a load of them up into the stratosphere where the cosmic rays could work on them. One of the mutations thereby produced had the ability to attack the human brain when the spores were inhaled and to destroy the victim's willpower. And now Bemis was broadcasting these mold spores all over the world so that he could take charge of Earth and order the inhabitants to do whatever he wished. And the man was mad.

Still, since Bemis and his assistants were not affected by the spores, there must be an antidote of some sort, and Bemis must keep it handy. If only he could force Bemis to tell where it was . . . , but that wasn't practical.

One of the men working on the balloons said, "Ten o'clock, Bert. Time to go for the mail."

"Won't be no mail, Jim boy. Everybody in Frederiksted's sitting around, looking dopey."

"Yeah, that's so. We ought to start organizing them before they all croak of starvation. We've got to have somebody to work for us."

"All right, smart guy, you go ahead and organize. Suppose you try to get the telephone service workin' again, while I have a smoke."

From beneath the house, Johnny saw one pair of booted legs disappear into the truck, which presently rolled out of the driveway. The other pair of legs settled themselves on the front steps.

Johnny remembered a sea almond tree behind the bungalow with a trunk that passed close to the eaves. Four minutes later, he padded silently across the roof and looked down on the smoker. As Bert threw away

18

his cigarette and stood up, Johnny's five hundred steel-muscled pounds landed on his back and flung him prone. Before he could fill his lungs to shout, the bear's paw landed with a *pop* on the side of his head. Bert quivered and subsided, his skull looking peculiarly lopsided.

Johnny listened; the house was quiet. But the man called Jim would soon be coming back in the truck. Johnny dragged the corpse under the house. Then, cautiously opening the screen door with his paws, he stole in, holding his claws up so that they would not click against the floor. He quickly located the room from which Bemis' voice wafted through the half-opened door.

Johnny slowly pushed the door open. The botanist's laboratory was full of flowerpots, glass cases of plants, and chemical apparatus. Bemis and the young Englishman were sitting at the far end, talking animatedly.

Johnny was halfway across the room before they saw him. They jumped up, Forney crying, "Good Gad!" Bemis gave one awful shriek as Johnny's right paw, working like an ice-cream scoop, tore into his abdomen. Bemis, now a horrible sight, tried to walk, then to crawl, then sank into a pool of his own blood.

Forney snatched up a chair, hoping to fend off Johnny like a lion tamer in a circus. Johnny, however, was not a lion. He rose five feet tall on his hind legs and batted the chair across the room, where it came to rest with a crash of glass. Forney broke for the door, but Johnny was on his back before he had gone three steps.

Johnny wondered how to dispose of Jim when he returned. The bear knew the man was armed, and he had a healthy dread of stopping another bullet. Then he noticed four automatic rifles in the umbrella stand in the hall. He opened the breech of one gun, found that it was loaded, then positioned himself behind a window that commanded a view of the driveway. When Jim got out of the truck, he never knew what hit him.

Johnny next set out to find the antidote for the spores. Bemis' desk seemed a logical place to start. Although the desk was locked and made of sheet steel, it was not designed to keep out a determined and resourceful bear. Johnny hooked his claws under the lowest drawer, braced himself, and heaved. The steel bent, and the drawer pulled forward. The others responded in turn. In the third drawer, he found a biggish squat bottle and two hypodermic syringes. Putting on his spectacles, he read "Potassium iodide."

This was the antidote, he decided, and it worked by injection. But how was a bear to work it? He carefully extracted the bottle stopper with his teeth and tried to fill one of the syringes. By holding the barrel of the device between his paws, and working the plunger with his mouth, he at last succeeded.

Carrying the syringe in his mouth, Johnny trotted back to the Station. He found Professor Mettin, still in his underwear, sitting in the kitchen dreamily eating the scraps left by the plug-uglies' raid. The others were utterly helpless without orders and would sit like vegetables until they starved.

Johnny tried to inject the solution into Mettin's calf, holding the syringe crosswise in his teeth and pushing the plunger with a paw. But at the prick of the needle, the man jerked away. When the bear held the man down, he squirmed so that the syringe broke.

A discouraged black bear cleaned up the broken glass. He knew that soon he would be the only thinking being left on Earth who had any initiative at all. He did not much care what happened to the human race, but he did have a certain affection for his lanky boss. Moreover, he didn't like the idea of spending the rest of his life rustling his own food like an ordinary wild animal. Such an existence would be far too dull for a bear of his intelligence.

So Johnny returned to Bemis' bungalow and brought back both the bottle and the remaining hypodermic syringe. He considered knocking one of the scientists unconscious and injecting him, but he did not know how hard to hit a human in order to stun without killing. He dared not try any rough stuff for fear of breaking the only remaining syringe.

Johnny sat down to think. Suddenly, he had an idea. In their present state, the humans would do anything they were told. If someone ordered one of them to pick up the syringe and inject himself, he would do it. But Johnny couldn't talk. His attempt to say "Pick up the syringe" came out as "Fee-feekopp feef-feef," and the Professor looked blankly away. Johnny put the syringe and precious chemical on a high shelf and started to roam through the rooms of the Research Station.

In Dr. Ryerson's room, he saw a typewriter. He couldn't handle a pencil, but he could, after a fashion, operate one of these machines. The chair creaked alarmingly under his weight as he took a piece of paper between his lips, dangled it over the machine, and turned the platen with both paws until the paper started through. The paper was in crooked, but that could not be helped. Using one claw at a time, he tapped out "PICK UP SIRINGE AND INJECT SOLUTION INTO YOUR ARM." The spelling of "siringe" didn't look quite right, but he couldn't be bothered with that now.

Carrying the paper in his mouth, he shuffled back into the kitchen. He placed the syringe in front of the Professor, squalled to attract his attention, and dangled the paper in front of his eyes. The scientist, completely dazed, paid no attention.

Johnny went out and walked around in the twilight, thinking furiously. It seemed absurd—even his bear's sense of humor told him so—that the spell could be broken by a simple command, that he alone in all the world knew the command, and that he had no way of giving it.

If the whole human race died off, leaving him the only intelligent creature on Earth, could he make his way to the mainland and seek out others of his species? Perhaps he could, but they, resenting his strangeness, might turn away from him or even kill him. That night he slept fitfully, knowing that time ran against him. He woke before dawn, thinking of Dr. Breuker's portable recording apparatus, though he could not imagine why.

He wandered into Breuker's room, found the tape recorder, and spent two hours learning how to operate the switches. He finally adjusted the thing for recording, yelled, "Wa-a-a-a-ah!" into it, threw the playback switch, and the machine yelled, "Wa-a-a-a-ah!" right back at him. Johnny squealed with pleasure.

Of course, a tape recording of his cry would be no better than his cry itself, but maybe among Breuker's tapes there might be some words he could use. He started to read the labels: "Bird cries," "Infant Babble," "Lancaster Dialect." He tried this latter tape and listened to a monologue about a little boy who was swallowed by a lion. From his experience with little boys, Johnny decided this would be a good idea, but there was nothing on the tape that would be of any use.

The next cassette he picked up was labeled "American Speech Series No. 72-B." It started out with a silly story: "Once there was a young rat who couldn't make up his mind. Whenever the other rats asked him if he'd like to come out with them, he'd answer, 'I don't know.' One day his aunt said to him, 'Now look here! No one will ever care for you if you carry on like this . . .' "

The player ground on, but Johnny's mind was made up. If he could get the machine to say "Now look here!" to Professor Mettin, his problem would be solved. He couldn't play the whole tape, because those three words did not stand out from the rest of the discourse. If he could make a separate recording of just those three words. . . . But how to do this? He needed two machines—one to play the tape and one to record the desired words. He squealed with exasperation. To be licked when he had gotten this far!

Like a flash, the solution came to him. He dragged the recorder over to the social room, where there was a small tape deck used by the scientists for their evening amusement. Johnny put the "American Speech" cassette in this machine, put a blank tape on the recorder, and started it. He kept a claw on the recorder switch to start the tape at just the right moment.

Two hours and several ruined tapes later, he had what he wanted. He nosed the recorder into the kitchen, laid the syringe and the typed paper in front of Mettin, and started the machine. It scraped along for ten seconds and then said sharply, "Now look here! Now look here! Now look here!" As the tape resumed its scraping, the Professor's eyes snapped back into focus. He looked intently at the sheet of paper with the single line of typing across it, and without a flicker of emotion, picked up the syringe and jabbed the needle into his biceps.

Johnny shut off the machine. He would have to wait to see whether the solution took effect. As the minutes passed, he had an awful feeling that maybe this was not the antidote after all.

A half hour later, Professor Mettin passed a hand across his forehead. His first words were barely audible, but they grew louder like a television set warming up. "What in heaven's name happened to me, Johnny? I remember everything that's taken place during the past three days, but I didn't seem to have any will of my own."

Johnny beckoned and headed for Ryerson's room and the typewriter. Mettin, who understood his Johnny, inserted a sheet of paper for him. Time passed as Johnny typed.

Finally, Mettin said, "What a sweet setup for a would-be dictator! With the whole world obeying orders implicitly, all he had to do was to select a few subordinates and have them give directions to everyone. Of course the antidote is potassium iodide—that's the standard fungicide. It cleared the mold out of my head in a hurry. Come on, old-timer, we've got a lot of work ahead of us. Hard to believe—a bear has saved the world!"

A week later everyone on St. Croix had been treated, and teams had set off for the mainland to carry on the mind-saving work.

Johnny, finding little to arouse his curiosity around the nearly deserted Biological Research Station, shuffled into the library. He took Volume 5 of the *Britannica* off the shelf, opened it to "Chemistry," and set to work again. He hoped Mettin would get back in a month or so to explain the hard parts to him. Meanwhile, he would have to wade through the article as best he could.

2

Old Man
Henderson

by
Kris Neville

"Joey, Joey," Mrs. Mathews sighed, "haven't I told you
and told you *not* to bring that animal in this house?"

"Awww, Mom," Joey said for what was probably the
hundredth time since his father had brought Jasper
home, "he won't hurt anything."

"I said, 'No,' and I mean just what I said! He st—
smells."

Joey ruffled the green feathers on Jasper's neck and
waited for the next line in the routine, which usually
went, with minor variations, "You just wait until your
father gets home, young man, and *then* you'll be sorry."
Joey always thought it a tremendously ineffective approach to the issue under consideration. His father
wouldn't be home from Mars for another three months
yet, and by that time, she would have forgiven—or at
least forgotten.

Today Mrs. Mathews, however, refused to run to her
usual form. She merely lowered her eyebrows, pursed
her lips, and glared at him.

Jasper squirmed around in Joey's arms until he could

look up at Mrs. Mathews with his big, bright, intelligent eyes, which were, at the moment, mildly reproachful.

Mrs. Mathews bolstered her relenting will. "You take him out of here this instant!"

Joey backed toward the door. "Can I play in the yard some more, then?"

Mrs. Mathews hid her enthusiasm for the idea behind sullen lips. "Well," she said, putting all the indecision she could muster into the syllable, "well, all right. For a little while longer. Then I want you to take a loaf of bread over to Old Man Henderson."

"Awww, Mom," Joey whined. He did not like Old Man Henderson.

"I don't see why," he said in his party voice, trying to keep from going too far with the overt expression of his resentment, "you have to bake bread anyway. No one else ever does."

She replied, in a very even voice, "I like homemade bread."

Joey debated a "Well, *I don't,*" which wasn't true, and wisely decided against it.

"Now take Jasper out of here, and let's have no more arguments."

"Yes, Mother," Joey said.

When Mrs. Mathews called Joey, an hour and a half later, the bread was fresh from the oven. There were six sweet-smelling, golden-brown loaves of it. The melted butter she had rubbed in made them glisten.

"Go wash your hands," she directed.

After he had left the room, she crossed to the cupboard, removed a section of plastic and wrapped the largest of the loaves tightly in it. Even through the insulation the bread felt delightfully warm in her hands. When you're as old as Old Man Henderson, she

27

told herself, the warm center of the bread, dripping with butter, ought to taste very good to you. She put the loaf in a plastic bag.

"Hurry, Joey!" she called.

"I'm coming. I'm *coming!*"

Shortly he came.

"Here. I want you to take this now, and hurry, so he can get it before it gets cold."

She always made a special point of that—to see that she sent out his loaf just as soon as the bread came out of the oven.

"Now, hurry," she admonished again.

It was no more than right, she told herself, that we do little things for poor Old Man Henderson once in a while. After all, it wasn't as if it were charity (which she vaguely disapproved of) because he did have the government pension; it was just to show that they really hadn't forgotten him.

"Can Jasper go with me?"

"Now, Joey . . ."

"Aw, gee, *please?*"

"Well, I don't know," she said indecisively. Old Man Henderson was so old, she reflected, that he probably wouldn't notice the odor, and some people really didn't mind at all.

Joey shifted his feet. "He won't mind," he encouraged. He wanted to add, "The way Old Man Henderson smells is a hundred times worse than Jasper."

"All right," Mrs. Mathews agreed slowly. "And hurry, now."

At the door, Joey turned. "Mother—If he wants me to stay a little while, may I?"

There! Mrs. Mathews reflected. That proved that if you raise a child properly (although at times he is bound to be exasperating beyond all measure and careless and

28

inconsiderate and thoughtless), he is sure to do the proper thing when he has the chance.

And with adults, too, it was the same: wanting to do the proper thing. Of course, you would expect adults to stop and visit with Old Man Henderson. "Here comes the Story down the street," they would say, and you knew immediately whom they meant. Although she, personally, would never say anything like that, or let anyone know how she really felt, she always found Old Man Henderson extremely tedious.

She smiled at her son. "But be sure to come back home in time for supper." She paused a fraction of a second and then added, "And, Joey—be a nice boy and remember, he's an old man, so don't tire him out."

"I'll remember," Joey promised.

As soon as he stepped out into the yard (letting the door slam after him), he called to his pet.

"Here, Jasper, here, boy! You want to come with me?"

Jasper appeared to consider the question. After a moment, he shuffled to his feet and flapped his wings. "Kweet-kweet," he said. He came at an awkward run.

"Well, let's go, then."

It took Joey better than two hours to get to Old Man Henderson's. The house was set back from the street, and it had a broad, well-kept lawn with islands of blooming flowers inset against the greenness of the grass.

Joey could remember how mad his father had been when, last Halloween, some of the neighborhood boys had littered it with little scraps of paper and pulled up all the flowers. It had taken Old Man Henderson nearly all day just to get the paper picked up. His father had said to Joey, "If a son of mine did a trick like that, I'd see to it he was whipped until he couldn't sit down."

And when his father discovered that Joey had helped to do it! Every time Joey thought about that, his bottom side prickled with the memory.

Joey stood on the porch for a long moment, wondering if it would be safe not to knock at all, but instead, throw the bread away somewhere and tell his mother he had delivered it. She would ask, "And how did he like the bread?" and he could reply, "Oh, he said to tell you that bakery bread couldn't come anywhere near yours." But Joey was a little afraid to risk a lie, so he knocked at the door.

After scarcely a second, Old Man Henderson called in his reedy voice, "Come in."

Reluctantly Joey opened the door and entered.

The room was dim—or perhaps it just seemed to Joey that it was dim, coming in fresh from the sunlight—and it smelled, as he knew it would, of the dry, sweet-acrid odor of age.

Old Man Henderson blinked. "Ah, ah," he said. "Come in, boy, and set a while." He tried to keep his voice casual to avoid betraying the fact that he had been sitting there all afternoon hoping one of his young friends would drop by to talk to him.

"I've brought you some fresh bread," Joey replied noncommittally.

"Ah, ah," Old Man Henderson said, "then you must be the Mathews boy." He had so many young friends that he sometimes confused their faces. There was the Jenkins lad, now, that looked a lot like this one.

"Well, well," he said, "so you've brought me some fresh bread, eh?"

"Yes."

"Ah, ah. Well, now, that's sure nice of you. Your mother makes fine bread. None better. Bakery bread

30

can't come anywhere near hers. Now you be sure to tell her I said that, will you?"

Joey grunted.

"You want to bet something, boy? I'll bet that she just now finished baking that bread. Every time she bakes, she sends me a loaf while it's still nice and hot. Your mother's a fine woman. You ought to be proud to have a mother like that."

Joey stared hard at the old man. "It's not hot this time," he said. "It's cold."

"Oh," Old Man Henderson said.

"Yes," he said, "she forgot all about it until it was already cold."

Old Man Henderson moved his jaw twice, blinked his eyes, and said, "Don't you worry about that. It'll taste just as good, anyway. Here. Give it to me, and I'll put it in the kitchen, there, for supper."

He took the bread and shuffled out of the room.

Joey wanted to leave before he got back, but he knew he should stay at least a little while, in case his mother should remark, "I hope Joey didn't tire you out, being over there all afternoon the other day." If he left too quickly, Old Man Henderson would be sure to remember that.

When the old man came back, he was carrying a little plate of crisp chocolate cookies with coconut toppings.

"Here," Old Man Henderson said. "Take these, now, and sit down over there. In the comfortable chair."

Joey took the cookies without saying anything and sat down.

Old Man Henderson sat down in another chair and studied the boy for a bit, trying to think of something to say.

"How are things, my little man?" he finally asked.

"Fine."

"Fine, eh? Well, well . . ."

Old Man Henderson looked down at his feet and then looked up again, waiting for Joey to say something else. When it became apparent that Joey had no intention of saying anything, Old Man Henderson reopened the conversation.

"You know," he began, "when you came in just a minute ago, I was sitting here thinking. . . . I was remembering back years and years ago. Must have been '51, '52 . . . yes, '52 . . . I believe it was. . . . Well, one time, and I wasn't much older than you, then . . ." He didn't think Joey was listening very attentively. "Well," he finished lamely, "never mind about all that."

Old Man Henderson realized that the long ago of his youth was not as real and vivid as yesterday's sunset except to himself, and that growing boys do not like to listen to an old man ramble about his childhood. What they like, he told himself, are adventure stories, tales of drama and excitement.

He peered at Joey.

Let's see, he reflected, have I told this one? . . . Nothing is worse, he frequently reminded himself, than an old man who harps continually on a single theme.

But after a moment's study, he was sure that he had never told this boy. Still, he didn't want to rush things. He would wait for a point at which the story would fall naturally into the conversation so that it wouldn't seem he was trying to force it on the boy.

For the first time (his eyes were not so good as they once were), Old Man Henderson noticed the strange animal that had entered with Joey. Less out of curiosity and more as a topic of conversation, he said, "Well, ah, ah . . . And what's that you've got there?" Of late he had ceased to care very much about the strange new things in the outside world.

"Huh? Oh, just Jasper."

"Jasper, eh? Well, well."

Joey had finished the cookies and now he felt more expansive. "Yes, Daddy brought him back from Venus." Joey scratched Jasper's head. "He's very intelligent and affectionate. And an ideal pet for children." Then he added emphatically, as if Old Man Henderson had disagreed, "Daddy says so!"

"Why, why, now that's fine. That's very fine. Well, well . . . Come here, Jasper."

Jasper peered up at Joey as if for permission and then scampered across the room.

Absently, Old Man Henderson reached down and ruffled Jasper's feathers. "I've sure never seen anything like this one."

Jasper hopped into his lap.

"My!" he said, beginning for the first time to take other than a conversational interest in the creature, for he always had a soft spot for affectionate animals. "Well, well. How do you like Old Man Henderson?"

Jasper nuzzled his hand and then looked up to study his face. "Kweeeeet," he said. He liked Old Man Henderson well enough.

"You should be very nice to him," the old man said.

"I am," Joey said. "Except once in a while. When he's mean."

"Ah, ah, yes," Old Man Henderson said.

Jasper had been following the conversation with his eyes and now, in the silence, he looked across at Joey.

At length, the old man said, "Ah, ah," half to himself. "Hummmm. Well. Venus you say?"

"Yes," Joey agreed. "We have to import food, and

that's very expensive, but Daddy says it's worth it if *I* like him."

"Ah, ah. Seems to me I remember reading about them—whatever-you-call-'ems—now that I come to think of it."

Joey narrowed his eyes. Just last week his mother had said, "It's a pity Old Man Henderson's too old to read anymore, with so many exciting things happening every day, things he's always dreamed of seeing happen."

"All right, then," Joey demanded, deleting an "if you know so much" at the last moment, "how do Kweets manage to live on Earth, where the air's so different?"

Old Man Henderson opened and shut his mouth. He was suddenly confused. He tried to remember about that article—it *was* just the other day when he was reading it, wasn't it?—but he could not. "Why, why," he said. "Ahhhhhh, ahhhhhhhhh—"

"See there! You don't know!" Joey cried triumphantly.

Old Man Henderson had been looking at the boy. Now, he looked away. He studied the back of his heavy, veined hand as it glided over Jasper's soft, green feathers. There was a puzzled, half-frightened look on his face.

"So your daddy gave him to you," he said at last. "And where is your daddy now?"

"He's on Mars, doing engineering on the new Dome. I'll bet I've told you that a hundred times!"

Old Man Henderson blinked twice as if someone had slapped him almost hard enough to bring tears. "Of course," he said hastily. "I remember, now. Mars, you say. I . . . I . . . I . . . ah, ah, Mars? Hummm."

He rubbed his withered hand along his leg.

"You know," he said, "when I was a young man, there

34

hadn't even been a man to the *moon.*" Already he could feel his confidence return. He had told the story quite a few times in the last fifty, seventy-five years. And he knew, too, that this young one would be sure to want to hear it, and that would make everything all right again. "A couple of people had circled around it, but nobody had ever *landed* on it."

"Well, well," said Joey.

No one ever addressed Old Man Henderson in that tone. People were always nice to him and listened politely. Now, he could not quite understand it. He looked down at Jasper for reassurance.

"Ah, ah, yes. There hadn't been a single man to the moon. . . . Well. You see that silver and gold plaque over the mantle, there?"

Joey did not turn to see.

But Old Man Henderson fell to studying it, and his eyes grew bright with the long-ago and faraway memory. Idly one of his hands stroked Jasper's sleek feathers.

"Do you know who gave that to me?" he asked.

"Yes," Joey said. "The President of the United States gave it to you."

Slowly Old Man Henderson's mind drifted back to the room. That had been his sentence, and it sounded harsh and frightening to hear it coming from young lips in a voice twisting all the glory of it into ashes. He could scarcely believe that he had heard correctly.

"Yes, yes, that's right," he heard his voice tell the boy, and it sounded weary and dry with disappointment.

"And I'll tell you why you got it," Joey said loudly. There was a queer excitement alive and throbbing in his body. He knew that the old man sitting before him was helpless before his words. He knew, also, that the old man would never protest to his mother. Not about this. It made him feel very big to be in a position to hurt

Old Man Henderson without danger to himself.

"You got it because you were the first man to land on the moon!"

Old Man Henderson felt ice form somewhere below his heart. He quit petting the Kweet and sat unseeing, listening, in spite of himself, to his own words come twisting back at him in cruel burlesque.

"I've heard that story I'll bet a hundred times! Now let me tell you about it. How it felt when you first saw the long steel ship"—Joey began to mimic the reedy voice of Old Man Henderson—*"glistening* in the Florida sunlight."

Old Man Henderson gestured weakly and wanted to ask the boy, please, to stop, but Joey did not give him the chance.

"And how it felt when you took off, acceleration pushing you back in your couch. And how it felt when you first saw the moon right there almost under your feet . . .

"And the celebration they gave the three of you when you got back, and how the President gave you that—that *thing* up there with his own two hands, and how he said—"

"Please, please. I meant no harm."

Joey had stopped for breath. He was incoherent with excitement.

"And how you had faith . . . ," and again his voice went to the upper register. " 'I always had *faith,* even when I was a little boy, that man couldn't be kept on Earth, that he was bound for the moon and then the planets and then the stars. I always had *faith!'*

"Nobody wants to listen to your silly old story anymore. Can't you see that! *Nobody wants to listen!* You've told it and told it until we're all sick and tired of hearing it!

"When they see you coming down the street, they say, 'Here comes Old Man Henderson and his Story!' and they *laugh* at you when your back's turned!"

Joey had to stop for breath.

Old Man Henderson made no sound.

In his excitement, Joey waved his arms wildly. He upset the cookie dish and it shattered on the floor. Joey began again, and it was almost a scream.

"You don't seem to realize that nobody wants to hear about how you went to the moon. Why, anybody can go to the moon! I've been there twice, and Daddy and Mama have both been to Venus, and Daddy's on Mars putting up a Dome right now so people can live in it, and it's going to be a bigger Dome than the one on Venus, and all you talk about is how you went to the moon!"

Joey was crying now.

"And you don't even know what a Kweet is, and you don't even know anything about what we're doing!"

He turned and ran to the door. There, he stopped and looked back. He saw Old Man Henderson sitting very still, not saying anything, and suddenly he didn't feel glad anymore.

"Come on, Jasper!" he screamed. "I'm getting out of here, away from that crazy old man!"

Jasper looked at Joey and said nothing. Then he turned his mute eyes to Old Man Henderson. He did not move.

For a moment, Joey did not know what to do; he began to feel the first rustlings of fear inside his mind. He turned and slammed the door behind him and began to run.

Jasper lay quietly in Old Man Henderson's lap. He looked up into the old face, the old face of loose folds of dry skin, but the face with the astonishingly bright eyes that brimmed with tears.

After a long time, Old Man Henderson put Jasper on the floor, stood up, and walked to Joey's chair. He got down on his knees and began to pick up pieces of the broken cookie dish.

Jasper walked over. "Kweet?" he asked very, very softly.

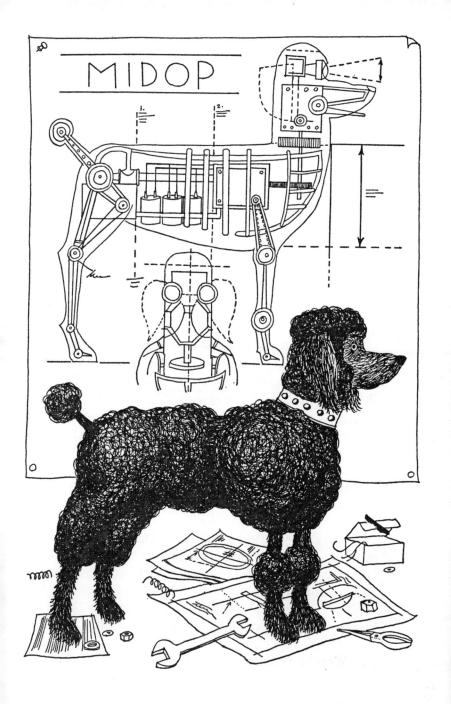

3

The
Million Dollar Pup

by
Catherine Crook de Camp

"Grandma, I want a dog," said Sally-Ann for the hundredth time. "I don't see why I can't have one."

"You can't have one because this is the twenty-first century, and dogs are not allowed in cities. That's why," replied Mrs. Barett once again. "Only the police have had dogs in New York since 2018."

Sally-Ann's grandmother paused, remembering. "Your mother was only four when they banned pets. I'll never forget how she cried and cried when they came and took her kitten away."

Mrs. Barett walked to the picture window of the apartment. Back in the 1980's, when the apartment house had been built, it had overlooked beautiful Central Park and housed only rich and famous people. Now the old woman stared out at the blank walls of enormous warehouses, which made Fifth Avenue a canyon thirty stories deep. The noise of traffic echoed and re-echoed. Lights from the heliport beyond the warehouses flashed on and off in the dusk of the short December day. Mrs. Barett sighed.

"Who banned pets?" Sally-Ann asked.

"The City Council, that's who," said Mrs. Barett. "They said there were over eighteen million animals in New York, all polluting the environment."

"And now they've cleaned up the air and the streets, so all we have is visual and auditory pollution. Big deal," said Sally-Ann bitterly. She brightened. "Hello, Mom," she said as her mother came into the room, shaking the snow off her scarf.

As Mrs. Turner slipped off her jacket and snow boots, Sally-Ann's grandmother spoke up. "You're home from work early, Maria, and a good thing it is. Sally-Ann's fussing again about a dog."

"For heaven's sake, Sally-Ann, what would we do with a dog in this small apartment, even if they let us have one?"

"Then why don't we move to the country, Mom? I want to see an evening star to wish on, and walk along roads with grass and trees and little houses. And I could have a puppy of my own."

"Oh, honey, you know we can't afford it." Mrs. Turner sat down wearily. "I've told you and told you that only rich folks live in the country. When your daddy left us and Grandpa died, we had to go on welfare. And the law says we've got to live wherever the welfare people tell us."

"But, Mom, you have a job, and Grandma's got social security."

"I know, Sally-Ann," said Mrs. Turner, "but it isn't enough. Besides, if we moved to the country, I couldn't keep my job in Brooklyn, now, could I?"

"I had a dog when I was a girl," put in Grandmother Barett, still thinking about the long-ago days. "I used to walk Kiki in Central Park. It was a fine park then—a little bit of country in the city. Kiki and I used to walk over the hills and around the lakes. Sometimes we even

41

walked through the children's zoo. It was a lovely place for a girl to walk her dog."

"Wish it had stayed that way," said Mrs. Turner.

"You both make me sick," burst out Sally-Ann, "talking and talking." She turned to glare at her mother. "All you want to do is stay here and take care of that crazy old man six days a week. Just baby-sitting a crazy old man!"

"Sally-Ann Turner, don't you go calling Dr. Silas Jones crazy. He's a kind man and a great inventor. An electronic wizard, that's what they called him. He still has a laboratory in the basement where he can fix anything he can see to fix and make it better than it was to begin with."

"What did he invent, Mom?"

"He was a robotic engineer in his younger days," Mrs. Turner said. "Tom, the old gardener who comes to cut the lawn and tend the flower beds, told me that Dr. Jones once invented a mechanical man who looked and acted real as real. It could walk, and talk, and even think like a human being. One whole summer he used it to open the door and serve the dinner."

"Seems unbelievable, doesn't it?" said Grandmother Barett. "There was nothing like that when I was a girl."

"If he's all that great, why isn't he inventing things now?" snapped Sally-Ann. "You keep saying he just sits there in his lab, doing nothing for hours and hours."

"I said he sits there thinking about new inventions. His mind is as sharp as ever; it's his eyesight that's failing. He tries to read those scientific reports he gets, but even with a magnifying glass, he can't read the fine print. The other day he got so mad at himself that he slammed the magnifier down on the desk and the handle came off. It took him two hours to fix it—fumbling, half-blind, with those miniature tools."

42

Grandmother Barett shook her head. "Poor soul," she said. "When the day comes that I can't read my paper and prayer book, I'll feel mighty lonesome."

"I don't see why," said Sally-Ann. "You could get all the news by watching the telecommunicator, even if you couldn't see the daily printouts. Reading is just a waste of time."

"Now, now," said Mrs. Turner mildly, "your English teacher would have a fit if she heard you say that. She would be sorry for every A she ever gave you. You know the stories you like to read don't come over the telecommunicator. Neither do the scientific journals Dr. Jones needs to keep up with the latest robotic discoveries."

"Humph!" said Sally-Ann. "When's dinner?"

That night Sally-Ann lay awake for a long time. She was more interested in the old inventor than she had let her mother see. An idea was taking shape in her mind: maybe he could make her a robot dog, a creature that could move like a dog, and think like a dog, and love its master, just like a dog, a real dog.

Sally-Ann knew that self-directed machines had done people's heavy and disagreeable work for over a hundred years. Way back in the 1950's, when computers first came into general use, the great science writer, Dr. Isaac Asimov, had set forth the three laws of robotics. Ever since, all well-intentioned robots had behaved according to these laws. Sally-Ann had learned the laws of robotics in her fifth-grade socioscience course. Now in the dark, she recited them aloud: "One: A robot may not injure a human being or, through inaction, allow a human being to come to harm. Two: A robot must obey orders given it by human beings, except when such orders would conflict with the First Law. Three: A

43

robot must protect its own existence, except when this conflicts with the First or Second Law."

Finally Sally-Ann drifted into a dream. She was standing beside a doctor in a meadow full of wild flowers. The doctor whistled through his fingers, as if summoning some animal. She noticed that his hands were lumpy and old but he used them cleverly. In answer to his call, a small dog bounded toward them. Putting its front paws against her leg, it looked up into her face. "We did it! We did it!" she shouted. The happy dog began to bark. But the barking turned into the buzz of a swarm of angry bees. Sally-Ann woke to the relentless buzzing of her alarm clock. It was time to get up and go to school.

As she dressed, Sally-Ann wondered about the old inventor. She had never before thought what it might be like to have an active mind imprisoned in a body that no longer worked very well. Grandma was old, of course, but not old like that. She could still take care of the apartment, go marketing, cook dinner, and read the newspaper printouts that spewed forth each morning and evening from their telecommunicator.

Sally-Ann tried to remember everything that her mother had ever said about Dr. Jones. She knew that he had all the materials he needed to go on inventing things and he had a brilliant mind. But he probably could not do delicate wiring or put together the microscopic electronic circuits that operated modern machines.

But she, Sally-Ann Turner, had exceptional motor control—they said that at school last fall when they gave her a complete physical exam. She had learned to handle tools. She could fix almost anything on vacuum cleaners and dishwashers, all without blowing a fuse or burning down the house. Even that embroidery and knitting her grandmother made her practice had accustomed her hands to fine work.

By the time she went to breakfast, Sally-Ann knew what she must do. Somehow or other, she must get into that laboratory of Dr. Jones's and learn all she could. Law or no law, she was going to have a pup, if she had to make it herself! In the meantime, she would try to play it smart.

At breakfast, she surprised her mother by saying sweetly, "Mom, I should like to go with you to your job next Saturday."

"Whatever for, honey?"

"I want to meet Dr. Jones and see his lab."

"But, Sally-Ann, he's not a science program on a TC show that you can sit and watch. He won't want to see you, like as not."

"I know, Mom, but I think he needs help, and I could read to him, and pick up after him in the lab, and—"

"Indeed you could not," her mother interrupted. "Nobody gets into that precious laboratory of his, not even me. He says there are valuable parts in there so small I might vacuum one up by mistake. Showed me one the other day no bigger than the tip of my smallest fingernail. Said that scrap of metal could make electrons travel like cars on a superhighway, and it would be priceless in the proper application—whatever that means."

"Sounds like crazy talk to me," said Grandma Barett.

Sally-Ann had to smile. "Grandma, that's not crazy talk. Dr. Jones is just using a *simile*—a figure of speech. You can often explain something by comparing it to something else. For instance, I could say 'You are *as thin as a rail,* but you eat *like a bird.'* "

"I'll be saying that to you, honey. If you don't hurry

up with that cereal, you'll be late for school."

"I'll hurry, Mom, but please let me go with you just once. I'm very good at reading aloud."

"I'll ask him today, but don't get your hopes up. He's kind of crotchety and doesn't like people much. Now run along, or you'll be late for sure."

Grinning broadly, Sally-Ann grabbed her coat and books and ran for the elevator. At least she had made it that far!

On Saturday morning, Sally-Ann and her mother boarded the underground auto-tram for Brooklyn. In historic Brooklyn Heights two-hundred-year-old houses with tall windows and arched doorways crowded along narrow, winding streets. Occasional gardens nestled behind stone walls. Through these open spaces, passersby could glimpse the wide harbor where the East River joined the Hudson. Sally-Ann, craning her neck, caught sight of the Statue of Liberty between the buildings.

At last they reached their stop.

"Well, here we are," said Mrs. Turner. "Now, mind your manners and don't pester Dr. Jones if he wants to be alone."

The tall limestone house wore the dignified air of a time when many city people owned their own homes and horse-drawn carriages clattered along the cobblestone streets.

"Gee, he must be very rich," said Sally-Ann as they waited for Dr. Jones to answer the doorbell.

"Be quiet, honey, here he is. Mr. Silas, sir, this is my daughter, Sally-Ann."

Sally-Ann was so astonished that she almost forgot to say, "Good morning, Dr. Jones. I'm pleased to meet you."

Dr. Jones was scarcely taller than Sally-Ann, which wasn't very tall. His white hair was rather long, and his skin was so transparent that networks of blood vessels formed a road map on his face. Yet his eyes, blazingly blue, examined her so competently that she could almost hear the click of his computerlike mind.

"Didn't expect me to look like this, eh?" he asked with a flicker of a smile. "Do come in, both of you, and, young lady, tell me what you did expect."

Sally-Ann gulped. "I thought you'd be big, and fat, and terribly important-looking, and . . . blind."

"Sally-Ann!" said Mrs. Turner, embarrassed. "I'm ashamed of—"

"Now, now, Mrs. Turner, there's a lot to be done upstairs. Don't you worry about us. We scientists have to tell the truth as we see it, don't we, young lady?"

Sally-Ann began to laugh. "I'm no scientist, Dr. Jones, but I'd sure like to see your lab. I'll be very careful about those . . . those integrated circuit chips of yours."

"Well, then, hang up your coat, take off your boots, and come with me."

Mrs. Turner, on her way to the second floor, stared in disbelief as her employer cheerfully led his young visitor down to his very private laboratory.

Sally-Ann was quiet on the way home in the dusk of that January day. Mrs. Turner had seen little of her daughter or her employer except when the three of them had lunched together in the high-ceilinged dining room overlooking the Hudson. Usually Dr. Jones ate his midday meal in his sitting room, but today he had suggested that the meal be served on a lace tablecloth set with silver candlesticks, sterling knives and forks, and his finest china plates.

"You've had a busy day, haven't you, honey?" asked Mrs. Turner as they reached the apartment door. "I heard you talking a blue streak in that lab and reading out loud in the sitting room."

"Yes, I was busy all right. Uncle Silas has a bunch of magazine articles to catch up on."

"*Uncle Silas,* Sally-Ann? You've got to be more respectful to the old. He's Dr. Jones to you."

"He's not all that old, Mom. In fact, he doesn't seem old at all. Besides, he *told* me to call him Uncle Silas."

"Are you certain sure, honey, he told you that?" asked her mother.

Sally-Ann nodded. "And I'm to come back next Saturday."

"Well, I never!" said Mrs. Turner as she unlocked the door to the apartment.

The Saturday visits to the house in Brooklyn Heights became a regular part of Sally-Ann's life. She learned a great deal from reading scientific articles, even though she often stumbled over strange words and unfamiliar concepts. Dr. Jones explained things to her and showed her how to handle the complicated tools on his workbench. With her nimble fingers, she soon learned how to solder almost invisible wires to tiny circuit chips with the sure touch of a professional lab worker.

Sally-Ann did all she could to please the old inventor. She tried to put herself in his place and guess what he would want almost before he knew himself. The longer she knew him, the more gentle and generous she found him. She began to feel a bit ashamed of her plan to find out all he knew and then build her own dog. Still, she continued to visit the house in Brooklyn Heights. She was enjoying herself, and Uncle Silas really seemed to need her.

One Saturday afternoon as the blustery March winds gave way to April breezes, Sally-Ann looked up from

48

the magazine article she was reading aloud. Now, if ever, was the time. She looked at Dr. Jones, took a long breath, and said, "Your gardener told my mother that you once invented a robot man that looked like a person instead of a machine. Is that the kind of thing you used to do?"

"Used to do, Sally-Ann? The word is *do*. Once an inventor, always an inventor. My field is robot development, as you know. Thirty-five years ago I designed the android ticket takers and security guards that still operate the metro auto-trams."

"You mean that the men and women who sell us tickets and keep us safe from pickpockets on the auto-tram platforms are just machines and you made them all here at the lab?"

"Oh, my, no. It takes over twenty large factories to turn out all the androids in use today. I designed the prototype, the first working model, and built it out of handmade parts. I had a partner in those days. His name was Colgate Curtis. C.C.'s now the president of the Sherman-Curtis Android Works."

Sally-Ann sat still so long that Dr. Jones asked, "Does it upset you that tram guards, and desk clerks, and waiters in restaurants are often not people at all but complicated, hard-working machines?"

"No, no. I was just thinking."

"About what, Missy?"

"About something I have to tell you," said Sally-Ann, "and I don't want to."

"Why not, my dear?"

"You won't like me anymore when I tell you. And I want you to like me. I really do." She felt hot tears well up in her eyes.

"Sally-Ann, I don't think there is anything you could say that would make me dislike you. You are thought-

49

ful, considerate, intelligent, and an excellent reader. What else could I want a friend to be?"

"Well," said Sally-Ann, "you could want me to be honest. I knew from the start that you had built an android; and I came here, not to be nice to you, but to learn how to build an android of my own."

"Now, why would you want to do that?" asked the old man.

"You see, I want a dog so badly and I got to thinking how I could build a machine that looks like a dog, and wags its tail like a dog, and goes for walks on a leash like a dog. I see now it wasn't fair. But, Uncle Silas, I want a puppy of my own so much—I've wanted one all my life, almost." The tears were flowing in earnest now.

"Sally-Ann! Sally-Ann!" Uncle Silas put his arm around her shoulders. "Don't you know it's all right to want something very, very much? That's how all great inventions begin. The inventor feels a want or sees a need and sets about to fulfill it."

Sally-Ann looked up. "Then you aren't mad at me? I truly love you even more than a silly old robot dog."

"Of course, of course. Here, take my handkerchief." As Sally-Ann dried her eyes, the old man walked over to the window and stared, unseeing, at the harbor.

"What a glorious idea—a robot dog—a *cynoid* I suppose we ought to call it."

"Cynoid! That's a funny word. Did you make it up?"

Dr. Jones smiled. " 'Cyno' is from the Greek word for 'dog,' and the suffix 'oid' means 'like.' So a cynoid is a doglike machine just as an android is a manlike machine. We scientists are always adapting Greek and Latin names for things, you know."

"Well, then, cynoid it is," said Sally-Ann. "Uncle Silas, will you make me my own cynoid, please?"

For a long moment, Dr. Jones studied his gnarled old hands. Then he shook his head. When he spoke, his voice was sad.

"I should have thought of that ten years ago, before my hands got stiff and my eyesight—"

"There's nothing wrong with your eyesight, Uncle Silas. You can see me perfectly well."

"Yes, my dear, but you are considerably larger than a line of print or a circuit chip for a transistor unit."

"Well, *my* eyesight's fine, and I'm getting good at microphotography and wiring. If you would just tell me what to do. . . . Couldn't we try? Please."

"I don't know. I just don't know. Let me think about it for a while. Just don't push me. Understand?"

Sally-Ann nodded.

Three weeks later, school let out for the summer. Still Dr. Jones said nothing. Sally-Ann spent more and more time reading aloud old scientific journals, typed notes, and handwritten memos from Dr. Jones's notebooks. Sometimes the old inventor would sit on the terrace with a faraway look in his eyes. At other times, he lay back in his reclining chair, hands folded over his stomach and eyes closed. Sally-Ann thought he was asleep, until one day he surprised her by snapping upright the moment she stepped into the doorway.

"Well, well, don't look so alarmed, my dear. I think I've found a possible solution to the problem of constructing a foreleg that bends when the animal takes its weight off a paw, while the hind legs have a reverse joint and move in an entirely different way. Head and tail movements and sound-box activation can be handled by basic wiring. Can't say the legs will work right, but we'll give it a try."

51

"I thought you'd forgotten all about . . . all about . . ." Sally-Ann stopped. She had no name for her mechanical puppy.

"Let's call her Midop—for Million Dollar Pup. If Midop works out, we'll both get rich."

"Get rich?" Sally-Ann stared at Uncle Silas in amazement. "Get rich on one cynoid made just for me?"

"Scratch that idea, Missy," said Dr. Jones. "I'm letting my dreams slip the leash. After all, we haven't built her yet, and maybe we never shall. Promise me you won't tell anyone what we're trying to do."

"Not even Mom or Grandma? Then who's going to sew the skin on Midop? And what will we use for skin?"

"Whoa! One question at a time." Dr. Jones tugged at his chin as he thought.

"For skin we could use a fur coat that's been up in the attic ever since Mrs. Jones died. It's black curly lamb, which goes back to the days when women wore coats made of the skins of real animals. Barbarous custom!"

"Then Midop will have to look like a poodle, with long legs and a square muzzle. Poodles have short curly hair."

"How do you know what a poodle looks like, Missy? Have you ever seen one?"

"Of course not, Uncle Silas. But I have a book showing all the different breeds of dog. I call it my dog-dreaming book."

"Fine. But we do have a real problem: who is to sew the skin on the prototype poodle? The project must remain a secret—a complete secret—until we file an application for a patent on the invention. Otherwise, Humanoid Robots, Ltd., is sure to steal our idea and market a cynoid first. They do that sort of thing all the time."

"Does it matter, Uncle Silas, as long as I have my pup?" asked Sally-Ann.

"Yes, indeed, it matters. The first person or company to patent a new invention with the United States Government gets the exclusive right, for seventeen years, to manufacture articles based on that patent. This means that no one else can use the invention without first getting the inventor's permission, and the inventor can get lots of money for giving his permission. That's why we must keep Midop a secret until we get a patent on her."

"But I can't sew and Grandma can," said Sally-Ann, frowning. "She worked in a fur coat factory when she was young. She could make Midop's skin look perfectly real."

"I'm sure she could, Missy. But can she keep a secret?"

"Oh, sure. Grandma and I often have secrets from Mom. Like when I'm rude while Mom's away or when I won't pick up my room."

"All right. We'll ask your grandmother when the time comes. Now let's get to work, Sally-Ann."

"Yes, Uncle Silas. I'm ready."

When the first leaves began to flutter down and scurry along the streets of Brooklyn Heights, Midop padded out of the laboratory. She was a small black poodle with an adorable tuft on her wagging tail and a yap that sent shivers of joy through Sally-Ann. When she walked up to a person, turned her pert little head to one side, wagged her tail and barked, she could melt the hardest heart.

Grandma Barett, needle and thread in hand, said, "My, isn't she the cutest thing!"

Dr. Jones said, "I like the way you clipped the fur around her paws and down her tail, like a show dog. And not a stitch shows."

Mrs. Turner said, "I can hardly believe it, Mr. Silas, sir. No one in a hundred years could guess she's not alive."

Sally-Ann said nothing. She was down on the floor, nose to nose with her pup, too happy to utter a word.

"Now, ladies," said the old inventor, "my doctor tells me I must take a two weeks' vacation whether I want to or not. While I'm gone, I shall leave the house in your charge. I suggest you all move in to guard the pup. Until the U.S. Patent Office notifies me that it has received my patent application, no one must know about the dog. We don't want Humanoid Robots to ruin our chances to make a mint of money, do we?"

Mother and daughter shook their heads. Grandma Barett whispered, "My, oh, my!"

Dr. Jones turned to Sally-Ann and said, "By the way, Missy, I'm leaving my Bermuda address here on the mantelpiece. Will you be sure to forward my mail until next Wednesday?"

"Yes, Uncle Silas, I'll be glad to. And thanks again for my beautiful puppy."

"I am glad you like her, Missy. Just remember to keep her in the laboratory until I get home two weeks from today."

Every afternoon during the two weeks of Dr. Jones's vacation, Sally-Ann would rush home from school to walk Midop around the laboratory. But the lab was small and cluttered for a frisky dog. Sally-Ann longed to take her poodle out into the open, to walk her properly on the fine rhinestone-studded leash that her grandmother had made.

54

By the second Friday, she could stand it no longer. She swung open the great front door and peered left and then right. The street was completely deserted. The sun was beginning to set, red in a pale-gold autumn sky. It would soon be dark, and there was no one to see them. She would only walk to the corner and back. Certainly, there was no harm in that. She ran back to the lab, tucked the poodle under her arm, grabbed her jacket, and stole down the front steps of the tall limestone house.

Once the harness was fastened around her furry body, Midop walked along the empty street, tugging at her leash in a most realistic way. Sally-Ann was so enchanted that she never noticed the approaching patrol car until it screeched to a stop and two burly police officers jumped out.

"What are you doing, Miss?" said the older officer sharply.

"Just walking," said Sally-Ann in a voice grown suddenly small.

"Don't you know it's against the law to walk a dog in New York? Where do you live?" The officer's voice was icy cold.

"I'm just visiting for a few days at Number 189, Dr. Silas Jones's house."

"You, Miss, and that animal will have to come down to the station house on Fulton Street and see the Captain."

"He won't hurt my dog, will he? He must not. He just can't." Sally-Ann began to cry.

"You'll be lucky if all they do is destroy the dog," said the older officer. "Your folks could be fined five hundred dollars for breaking the law."

The younger policeman seemed kinder as he asked, "What is your name and where are your folks?"

"I'm Sally-Ann Turner. Mom's at the supermarket, but Grandma is at Number 189, over there."

"Get in the car," said the older officer. "We'll pick up your grandmother and take both of you to headquarters."

Fifteen minutes later, a trembling girl, clutching her poodle, and a worried old woman stood in front of the precinct police captain. He asked a hundred questions —or so it seemed—of both Sally-Ann and Mrs. Barett.

"Name? Age? Present address? Permanent address? Where did you get that dog?"

Then turning to Mrs. Barett, the Captain said, "Didn't you know about the New York City ordinance against pets? You've lived here all your life! Anyway, ignorance of the law is no excuse." He glared at the woman angrily.

"Yes, I know the law, sir," answered Mrs. Barett. "But the dog—"

"Call the Commissioner," ordered the Captain, "and get hold of a reporter from the *Times.* Violations like this must receive wide publicity to deter similar infractions."

Sally-Ann thought frantically. If the police thought Midop was a live animal, they would destroy her. If they learned that she was a cynoid, newspaper and telecommunication reports would be all over town by morning. And Dr. Jones didn't have the receipt from Washington that would protect his invention.

Even if they kill me, she thought, I'll never tell them that my pup is a machine. Someday, Dr. Jones may build another dog with someone else to help him.

An endless hour later, the Police Commissioner, a reporter, and a cameraman arrived at the precinct headquarters. Pictures were taken of Sally-Ann holding her poodle while a beetle-browed Commissioner shook his finger at her.

"The dog must be destroyed immediately," he said, "and the lawbreakers shall spend the night in jail."

Sally-Ann turned white and bolted for the door. Blue-coated arms caught her before she had crossed the room.

"Run, Midop, run," she cried, tossing the little animal toward the long corridor that led to the station house doorway. Even as the police officer dragged her back to the Captain's desk, she heard her grandmother's voice rising in a room that had grown very quiet.

"That pup isn't a real dog, Your Honor, sir. It's a mechanical toy. Dr. Silas Jones built it out of electrical parts; that's what makes it walk and wag and bark. I sewed the fur on it with my own two hands."

"A likely story. Don't lie to me," thundered the Commissioner. To the Captain he added, "Order your handler to bring in a guard dog before that wretched creature gets away."

Sally-Ann, sobbing loudly beside a policeman, saw Midop futilely push her paws against the heavy oaken doors. She saw the photographer rush down the hall. For a wild moment, she thought that he was going to help Midop escape. But when he came close, he slid to one knee and positioned the camera to record the kill.

It all happened so fast that she hardly noticed the huge, wolflike beast that trotted into the room on a heavy chain until his handler bent down, snapped off the leash, and commanded, "Attack."

Sally-Ann screamed. The police dog gathered his mighty haunches under him and bounded down the hall, fangs bared to seize the black poodle. A foot away, he stopped abruptly and began sniffing Midop in a puzzled fashion. Then, growling uncertainly, he sat at attention with a canine frown on his intelligent face. Midop stopped pawing at the door, faced the ferocious animal, and wagged her tail. Nobody spoke for thirty seconds.

"You see, sir, I don't tell lies," said Grandmother Barett. "The pup's a toy; and no dog here at the station, if he's like any dog I ever knew, would give a second sniff to a toy dog. Dogs know a real dog when they meet one, even if humans don't."

The Commissioner looked displeased and just a trifle foolish.

"Captain," he said, "next time make damn sure of your facts before calling me away from my dinner. And you," he added, glaring at the reporter and photographer, "no mention of my being here tonight and no pictures of me—understand? Make a mistake and you'll get no more police stories in this city—ever."

As soon as the Commissioner had slammed the door behind him, the Captain turned a grim face toward Sally-Ann and her grandmother.

"I ought to lock you up for disturbing the peace," he sputtered. "Now get out of here as fast as you can—you and your stupid toy dog."

Without another word, Sally-Ann shakily gathered Midop into her arms and, followed by her grandmother, left the precinct headquarters. As they stood on the steps outside, they were joined by the *Times* reporter and his cameraman.

"You'll see yourself and your pup on page one tomorrow morning, young lady," said the reporter, smiling.

"Please don't, oh, please, please don't," wailed Sally-Ann in vain.

"There's nothing to be afraid of now, girlie," the reporter said. "It will make a fine human interest story—

a girl and her robot dog. Every kid in the city will be wanting one too."

Although she went to bed early, Sally-Ann hardly slept. She wondered whether Uncle Silas could ever forgive her for disobeying his orders. Downstairs in the parlor, her mother and grandmother walked the floor for hours. They worried about what the loss of the invention might do to Dr. Jones.

"He won't have anything to live for now," said Mrs. Turner.

"Poor soul," said Mrs. Barett, "just when everything was going right for him."

At eleven o'clock the next morning, a taxi bearing the returning inventor drew up to the house in Brooklyn Heights. Three worried people lined up in the hall and silently opened the great front door.

"What's the matter, ladies?" boomed Dr. Jones. His unexpected cheerfulness turned a knife in every heart.

"Have you seen the morning *Times,* sir?" asked Mrs. Turner anxiously, while Sally-Ann twisted and untwisted her fingers.

"Why, yes. Yes indeed. A wonderful write-up about Midop and an excellent picture of Sally-Ann holding the dog. We couldn't *buy* city-wide coverage like that for love or money."

"I thought . . . I thought—" began Mrs. Turner.

"That you'd be real upset by Sally-Ann's escapade," finished Mrs. Barett.

Sally-Ann, eyes big as saucers, had nothing at all to say.

"Why did you think that, Mrs. Turner? Mrs. Barett?"

"Because of that company stealing your invention before the receipt for the pattern came from Washington," said Mrs. Barett.

59

"Oh, you mean the receipt for the *patent* application. Why, that was sent the day after I left for Bermuda, and Missy forwarded it along with my other mail."

"Did I, Uncle Silas?" asked Sally-Ann.

"Indeed you did, my dear. Here are the papers." Uncle Silas drew a large document out of his breast pocket. "See, it says: To Silas Jones and Sally-Ann Turner: Patent Number 11,568,094. And this," he added, unfolding another document, "is a contract that I have made with Sherman-Curtis to manufacture the cynoid under our patent. It is all ready for your signature and that of your mother as guardian."

"Does this mean that city children all over America will have their own puppies again?" Sally-Ann's eyes shone like the evening star.

"Yes, indeed, Missy. And you and I shall have plenty of money. How would you ladies like to move in with me? This old house is large enough for all of us and Midop too."

4

The
Smallest Dragonboy

by
Anne McCaffrey

Although Keevan lengthened his walking stride as far as his legs would stretch, he couldn't quite keep up with the other candidates. He knew he would be teased again.

Just as he knew many other things that his foster-mother told him he ought not to know, Keevan knew that Beterli, the most senior of the boys, set that spanking pace just to embarrass him, the smallest dragonboy. Keevan would arrive, tail fork-end of the group, breathless, chest heaving, and maybe get a stern look from the instructing wingsecond.

Dragonriders, even if they were still only hopeful candidates for the glowing eggs that were hardening on the hot sands of the Hatching Ground cavern, were expected to be punctual and prepared. Sloth was not tolerated by the weyrleader of Benden Weyr. A good record was especially important now. It was very near hatching time, when the baby dragons would crack their mottled shells and stagger forth to choose their lifetime companions. The very thought of that glorious moment made Keevan's breath catch in his throat. To be chosen—to be a dragonrider! To sit astride the neck of the winged beast with the jeweled eyes, to be his friend in telepathic communion with him for life, to be his companion in good times and fighting extremes, to fly effortlessly over the lands of Pern! Or, thrillingly, *between* to any point anywhere on the world! Flying *between* was done on dragonback or not at all, and it was dangerous.

Keevan glanced upward, past the black mouths of the weyr caves in which grown dragons and their chosen riders lived, toward the Star Stones that crowned the ridge of the old volcano that was Benden Weyr. On the height, the blue watch dragon, his rider mounted on his neck, stretched the great transparent pinions that carried him on the winds of Pern to fight the evil Thread that fell at certain times from the sky. The many-faceted rainbow jewels of his eyes glistened momentarily in the greeny sun. He folded his great wings to his back, and the watchpair resumed their statuesque pose of alertness.

Then the enticing view was obscured as Keevan passed into the Hatching Ground cavern. The sands underfoot were hot, even through heavy wher-hide boots. How the bootmaker had protested having to sew so small! Keevan was forced to wonder again why being small was reprehensible. People were always calling him "babe" and shooing him away as being "too small" or "too young" for this or that. Keevan was constantly working, twice as hard as any other boy his age, to prove himself capable. What if his muscles weren't as big as Beterli's? They were just as hard. And if he couldn't overpower anyone in a wrestling match, he could outdistance everyone in a footrace.

"Maybe if you run fast enough," Beterli had jeered on the occasion when Keevan had been goaded to boast of his swiftness, "you could catch a dragon. That's the only way you'll make a dragonrider!"

"You just wait and see, Beterli, you just wait," Keevan had replied. He would have liked to wipe the contemptuous smile from Beterli's face, but the guy didn't fight fair even when the wingsecond was watching. "No one knows what Impresses a dragon!"

"They've got to be able to *find* you first, babe!"

Yes, being the smallest candidate was not an enviable position. It was therefore imperative that Keevan Impress a dragon in his first hatching. That would wipe the smile off every face in the cavern and accord him the respect due any dragonrider, even the smallest one.

Besides, no one knew exactly what Impressed the baby dragons as they struggled from their shells in search of their lifetime partners.

"I like to believe that dragons see into a man's heart," Keevan's foster-mother, Mende, told him. "If they find goodness, honesty, a flexible mind, patience, courage—and you've that in quantity, dear Keevan—that's what dragons look for. I've seen many a well-grown lad left standing on the sands, Hatching Day, in favor of someone not so strong or tall or handsome. And if my memory serves me" (which it usually did—Mende knew every word of every Harper's tale worth telling, although Keevan did not interrupt her to say so), "I don't believe that F'lar, our weyrleader, was all that tall when bronze Mnementh chose him. And Mnementh was the only bronze dragon of that hatching."

Dreams of Impressing a bronze were beyond Keevan's boldest reflections, although that goal dominated the thoughts of every other hopeful candidate. Green dragons were small and fast and more numerous. There was more prestige to Impressing a blue or a brown than a green. Being practical, Keevan seldom dreamed as

64

high as a big fighting brown, like Canth, F'nor's fine fellow, the biggest brown on all Pern. But to fly a bronze? Bronzes were almost as big as the queen, and only they took the air when a queen flew at mating time. A bronze rider could aspire to become weyrleader! Well, Keevan would console himself, brown riders could aspire to become wingseconds, and that wasn't bad. He would even settle for a green dragon: they were small, but so was he. No matter! He simply had to Impress a dragon his first time in the Hatching Ground. Then no one in the weyr would taunt him anymore for being so small.

Shells, thought Keevan now, but the sands are hot!

"Impression time is imminent, candidates," the wingsecond was saying as everyone crowded respectfully close to him. "See the extent of the striations on this promising egg." The stretch marks *were* larger than yesterday.

Everyone leaned forward and nodded thoughtfully. That particular egg was the one Beterli had marked as his own, and no other candidate dared, on pain of being beaten by Beterli on the first opportunity, to approach it. The egg was marked by a large yellowish splotch in the shape of a dragon backwinging to land, talons outstretched to grasp rock. Everyone knew that bronze eggs bore distinctive markings. And naturally, Beterli, who had been presented at eight Impressions already and was the biggest of the candidates, had chosen it.

"I'd say that the great opening day is almost upon us," the wingsecond went on, and then his face assumed a grave expression. "As we well know, there are only forty eggs and seventy-two candidates. Some of you may be disappointed on the great day. That doesn't necessarily mean you aren't dragonrider material, just that *the* dragon for you hasn't been shelled. You'll have

65

other hatchings, and it's no disgrace to be left behind an Impression or two. Or more."

Keevan was positive that the wingsecond's eyes rested on Beterli, who had been stood off at so many Impressions already. Keevan tried to squinch down so the wingsecond wouldn't notice him. Keevan had been reminded too often that he was eligible to be a candidate by one day only. He, of all the hopefuls, was most likely to be left standing on the great day. One more reason why he simply had to Impress at his first hatching.

"Now move about among the eggs," the wingsecond said. "Touch them. We don't know that it does any good, but it certainly doesn't do any harm."

Some of the boys laughed nervously, but everyone immediately began to circulate among the eggs. Beterli stepped up officiously to "his" egg, daring anyone to come near it. Keevan smiled, because he had already touched it . . . every inspection day . . . as the others were leaving the Hatching Ground, when no one could see him crouch and stroke it.

Keevan had an egg he concentrated on, too, one drawn slightly to the far side of the others. The shell bore a soft greenish-blue tinge with a faint creamy swirl design. The consensus was that this egg contained a mere green, so Keevan was rarely bothered by rivals. He was somewhat perturbed then to see Beterli wandering over to him.

"I don't know why you're allowed in this Impression, Keevan. There are enough of us without a babe," Beterli said, shaking his head.

"I'm of age." Keevan kept his voice level, telling himself not to be bothered by mere words.

"Yah!" Beterli made a show of standing on his toe tips. "You can't even see over an egg. Hatching Day, you better get in front or the dragons won't see you at all. Course, you could get run down that way in the mad scramble. Oh, I forget, you can run fast, can't you?"

"You'd better make sure a dragon sees *you*, this time, Beterli," Keevan replied. "You're almost overage, aren't you?"

Beterli flushed and took a step forward, hand half raised. Keevan stood his ground, but if Beterli advanced one more step, he would call the wingsecond. No one fought in the Hatching Ground. Surely Beterli knew that much.

Fortunately, at that moment the wingsecond called the boys together and led them from the Hatching Ground to start on evening chores.

There were "glows" to be replenished in the main kitchen caverns and sleeping cubicles, the major hallways, and the queen's apartment. Firestone sacks had to be filled against Thread attack, and black rock brought to the kitchen hearths. The boys fell to their chores, tantalized by the odors of roasting meat. The population of the weyr began to assemble for the evening meal, and the dragonriders came in from the Feeding Ground or their sweep checks.

It was the time of day Keevan liked best: once the chores were done, before dinner was served, a fellow could often get close to the dragonriders and listen to their talk. Tonight Keevan's father, K'last, was at the main dragonrider table. It puzzled Keevan how his father, a brown rider and a tall man, could *be* his father —because he, Keevan, was so small. It obviously never puzzled K'last when he deigned to notice his small son: "In a few more turns, you'll be as tall as I am—or taller!"

K'last was pouring Benden drink all around the table. The dragonriders were relaxing. There would be no Thread attack for three more days, and they would be in the mood to tell tall tales, better than Harper yarns, about impossible maneuvers they had done a-dragonback. When Thread attack was closer, their talk would change to a discussion of tactics of evasion, of going *between,* how long to suspend there until the burning but fragile Thread would freeze and crack and fall harmlessly off dragon and man. They would dispute the exact moment to feed firestone to the dragon so he would have the best flame ready to sear Thread midair and render it harmless to ground—and man—below. There was such a lot to know and understand about being a dragonrider that sometimes Keevan was overwhelmed. How would he ever be able to remember everything he ought to know at the right moment? He couldn't dare ask such a question; this would only have given additional weight to the notion that he was too young yet to be a dragonrider.

"Having older candidates makes good sense," L'vel was saying, as Keevan settled down near the table. "Why waste four to five years of a dragon's fighting prime until his rider grows up enough to stand the rigors?" L'vel had Impressed a blue of Ramoth's first clutch. Most of the candidates thought L'vel was marvelous because he spoke up in front of the older riders, who awed them. "That was well enough in the Interval when you didn't need to mount the full weyr complement to fight Thread. But not now. Not with more eligible candidates than ever. Let the babes wait."

"Any boy who is over twelve turns has the right to stand in the Hatching Ground," K'last replied, a slight smile on his face. He never argued or got angry. Keevan wished he were more like his father. And oh, how he wished he were a brown rider! "Only a dragon . . . each particular dragon . . . knows what he wants in a rider. We certainly can't tell. Time and again the theorists"—and K'last's smile deepened as his eyes swept those at the table—"are surprised by dragon choice. *They* never seem to make mistakes, however."

"Now, K'last, just look at the roster this Impression. Seventy-two boys and only forty eggs. Drop off the twelve youngest, and there's still a good field for the hatchlings to choose from. Shells! There are a couple of weyrlings unable to see over a wher egg, much less a dragon! And years before they can ride Thread."

"True enough, but the weyr is scarcely under fighting strength, and if the youngest Impress, they'll be old enough to fight when the oldest of our current dragons go *between* from senility."

"Half the weyrbred lads have already been through several Impressions," one of the bronze riders said then. "I'd say drop some of *them* off this time. Give the untried a chance."

"There's nothing wrong in presenting a clutch with as wide a choice as possible," said the weyrleader, who had joined the table with Lessa, the weyrwoman.

"Has there ever been a case," she said, smiling in her odd way at the riders, "where a hatchling didn't choose?"

Her suggestion was almost heretical and drew astonished gasps from everyone, including the boys.

F'lar laughed. "You say the most outrageous things, Lessa."

"Well, *has* there ever been a case where a dragon didn't choose?"

"Can't say as I recall one," K'last replied.

"Then we continue in this tradition," Lessa said firmly, as if that ended the matter.

But it didn't. The argument ranged from one table to the other all through dinner, with some favoring a weeding out of the candidates to the most likely, lopping off those who were very young or who had had multiple opportunities to Impress. All the candidates were in a swivet, though such a departure from tradition would be to the advantage of many. As the evening progressed, more riders were favoring eliminating the youngest and those who had passed four or more Impressions unchosen. Keevan felt he could bear such a dictum if only Beterli was also eliminated. But this seemed less likely than that Keevan would be tuffed out, since the weyr's need was for fighting dragons and riders.

By the time the evening meal was over, no decision had been reached, although the weyrleader had promised to give the matter due consideration.

He might have slept on the problem, but few of the candidates did. Tempers were uncertain in the sleeping caverns next morning as the boys were routed out of their beds to carry water and black rock and cover the "glows." Mende had to call Keevan to order twice for clumsiness.

"Whatever is the matter with you, boy?" she demanded in exasperation when he tipped black rock short of the bin and sooted up the hearth.

"They're going to keep me from this Impression."

"What?" Mende stared at him. "Who?"

"You heard them talking at dinner last night. They're going to tuff the babes from the hatching."

Mende regarded him a moment longer before touching his arm gently. "There's lots of talk around a supper table, Keevan. And it cools as soon as the supper. I've heard the same nonsense before every hatching, but nothing is ever changed."

"There's always a first time," Keevan answered, copying one of her own phrases.

"That'll be enough of that, Keevan. Finish your job.

70

If the clutch does hatch today, we'll need full rock bins for the feast, and you won't be around to do the filling. All my fosterlings make dragonriders."

"The first time?" Keevan was bold enough to ask as he scooted off with the rockbarrow.

Perhaps, Keevan thought later, if he hadn't been on that chore just when Beterli was also fetching black rock, things might have turned out differently. But he had dutifully trundled the barrow to the outdoor bunker for another load just as Beterli arrived on a similar errand.

"Heard the news, babe?" asked Beterli. He was grinning from ear to ear, and he put an unnecessary emphasis on the final insulting word.

"The eggs are cracking?" Keevan all but dropped the loaded shovel. Several anxieties flicked through his mind then; he was black with rock dust—would he have time to wash before donning the white tunic of candidacy? And if the eggs were hatching, why hadn't the candidates been recalled by the wingsecond?

"Naw! Guess again!" Beterli was much too pleased with himself.

With a sinking heart Keevan knew what the news must be, and he could only stare with intense desolation at the older boy.

"C'mon! Guess, babe!"

"I've no time for guessing games," Keevan managed to say with indifference. He began to shovel black rock into his barrow as fast as he could.

"I said 'guess.' " Beterli grabbed the shovel.

"And I said I'd no time for guessing games."

Beterli wrenched the shovel from Keevan's hands. "Guess!"

"I'll have the shovel back, Beterli." Keevan straightened up, but he didn't come up to Beterli's bulky shoulder. From somewhere, other boys appeared, some with barrows, some mysteriously alerted to the prospect of a confrontation among their numbers.

"Babes don't give orders to candidates around here, babe!"

Someone sniggered and Keevan knew, incredibly, that he must have been dropped from the candidacy.

He yanked the shovel from Beterli's loosened grasp. Snarling, the older boy tried to regain possession, but Keevan clung with all his strength to the handle, dragged back and forth as the stronger boy jerked the shovel about.

With a sudden, unexpected movement, Beterli rammed the handle into Keevan's chest, knocking him over the barrow handles. Keevan felt a sharp, painful jab behind his left ear, an unbearable pain in his right shin, and then a painless nothingness.

Mende's angry voice roused him, and startled, he tried to throw back the covers, thinking he had overslept. But he couldn't move, so firmly was he tucked into his bed. And then the constriction of a bandage on his head and the dull sickishness in his leg brought back recent occurrences.

"Hatching?" he cried.

"No, lovey," said Mende, and her voice was suddenly very kind, her hand cool and gentle on his forehead. "Though there's some as won't be at any hatching again." Her voice took on a stern edge.

Keevan looked beyond her to see the weyrwoman, who was frowning with irritation.

"Keevan, will you tell me what occurred at the black-rock bunker?" Lessa asked, but her voice wasn't angry.

He remembered Beterli now and the quarrel over the shovel and . . . what had Mende said about some not being at any hatching? Much as he hated Beterli, he couldn't bring himself to tattle on Beterli and force him out of candidacy.

"Come, lad," and a note of impatience crept into the weyrwoman's voice. "I merely want to know what happened from you, too. Mende said she sent you for black rock. Beterli—and every weyrling in the cavern—seems to have been on the same errand. What happened?"

"Beterli took the shovel. I hadn't finished with it."

"There's more than one shovel. What did he *say* to you?"

"He'd heard the news."

"What news?" The weyrwoman was suddenly amused.

"That . . . that . . . there'd been changes."

"Is that what he said?"

"Not exactly."

"What did he say? C'mon, lad. I've heard from everyone else, you know."

"He said for me to guess the news."

"And you fell for that old gag?" The weyrwoman's irritation returned.

"Consider all the talk last night at supper, Lessa," said Mende. "Of course the boy would think he'd been eliminated."

"In effect, he is, with a broken skull and leg." She touched his arm, a rare gesture of sympathy in her. "Be that as it may, Keevan, you'll have other Impressions. Beterli will not. There are certain rules that must be observed by all candidates, and his conduct proves him unacceptable to the weyr."

She smiled at Mende and then left.

"I'm still a candidate?" Keevan asked urgently.

"Well, you are and you aren't, lovey," his foster-mother said. "Is the numb weed working?" she asked,

73

and when he nodded, she said, "You just rest. I'll bring you some nice broth."

At any other time in his life, Keevan would have relished such cosseting, but he lay there worrying. Beterli had been dismissed. Would the others think it was his fault? But everyone was there! Beterli had provoked the fight. His worry increased, because although he heard excited comings and goings in the passageway, no one tweaked back the curtain across the sleeping alcove he shared with five other boys. Surely one of them would have to come in sometime. No, they were all avoiding him. And something else was wrong. Only he didn't know what.

Mende returned with broth and beachberry bread.

"Why doesn't anyone come see me, Mende? I haven't done anything wrong, have I? I didn't ask to have Beterli tuffed out."

Mende soothed him, saying everyone was busy with noontime chores and no one was mad at him. They were giving him a chance to rest in quiet. The numb weed made him drowsy, and her words were fair enough. He permitted his fears to dissipate. Until he heard the humming. It started low, too low to be heard. Rather he felt it in the broken shinbone and his sore head. And thought, at first, it was an effect of the numb weed. Then the hum grew, augmented by additional sources. Two things registered suddenly in Keevan's groggy mind: the only white candidate's robe still on the pegs in the chamber was his, and dragons hummed when a clutch was being laid or being hatched. Impression! And he was flat abed.

Bitter, bitter disappointment turned the warm broth sour in his belly. Even the small voice telling him that he would have other opportunities failed to alleviate his crushing depression. *This* was the Impression that mat-

74

tered! This was his chance to show *everyone* from Mende to K'last to L'vel and even the weyrleaders that he, Keevan, was worthy of being a dragonrider.

He twisted in bed, fighting against the tears that threatened to choke him. Dragonmen don't cry! Dragonmen learn to live with pain. . . .

Pain? The leg didn't actually pain him as he rolled about on his bedding. His head felt sort of stiff from the tightness of the bandage. He sat up, an effort in itself since the numb weed made exertion difficult. He touched the splinted leg, but the knee was unhampered. He had no feeling in his bone, really. He swung himself carefully to the side of his bed and slowly stood. The room wanted to swim about him. He closed his eyes, which made the dizziness worse, and he had to clutch the bedpost.

Gingerly he took a step. The broken leg dragged. It hurt in spite of the numb weed, but what was pain to a dragonman?

No one had said he couldn't go to the Impression. "You are and you aren't," were Mende's exact words.

Clinging to the bedpost, he jerked off his bedshirt. Stretching his arm to the utmost, he jerked his white candidate's tunic from the peg. Jamming first one arm and then the other into the holes, he pulled it over his head. Too bad about the belt. He couldn't wait. He hobbled to the door, hung on to the curtain to steady himself. The weight on his leg was unwieldy. He would not get very far without something to lean on. Down by the bathing pool was one of the long crook-necked poles used to retrieve clothes from the hot washing troughs. But it was down there, and he was on the level above. And there was no one nearby to come to his aid —everyone would be in the Hatching Ground right now, eagerly waiting for the first egg to crack.

75

The humming increased in volume and tempo, an urgency to which Keevan responded, knowing that his time was all too limited if he was to join the ranks of the hopeful boys standing around the cracking eggs. But if he hurried down the ramp, he would fall flat on his face.

He could, of course, go flat on his rear end, the way crawling children did. He sat down, the jar sending a stab of pain through his leg and up to the wound on the back of his head. Gritting his teeth and blinking away the tears, Keevan scrabbled down the ramp. He had to wait a moment at the bottom to catch his breath. He got to one knee, the injured leg straight out in front of him. Somehow, he managed to push himself erect, though the room wanted to tip over his ears. It wasn't far to the crooked stick, but it seemed an age before he had it in his hand.

Then the humming stopped!

Keevan cried out and began to hobble frantically across the cavern, out to the bowl of the weyr. Never had the distance between the living caverns and the Hatching Ground seemed so great. Never had the weyr been so silent, breathless. As if the multitude of people and dragons watching the hatching held every breath in suspense. Not even the wind muttered down the steep sides of the bowl. The only sounds to break the stillness were Keevan's ragged breathing and the *thump-thud* of his stick on the hard-packed ground. Sometimes he had to hop twice on his good leg to maintain his balance. Twice he fell into the sand and had to pull himself up on the stick, his white tunic no longer spotless. Once he jarred himself so badly he couldn't get up immediately.

Then he heard the first exhalation of the crowd, the ooohs, the muted cheer, the susurrus of excited whispers. An egg had cracked, and the dragon had chosen his rider. Desperation increased Keevan's hobble. Would he never reach the arching mouth of the Hatching Ground?

Another cheer and an excited spate of applause spurred Keevan to greater effort. If he didn't get there in moments, there would be no unpaired hatchling left. Then he was actually staggering into the Hatching Ground, the sands hot on his bare feet.

No one noticed his entrance or his halting progress. And Keevan could see nothing but the backs of the white-robed candidates, seventy of them ringing the area around the eggs. Then one side would surge forward or backward and there would be a cheer. Another dragon had been Impressed. Suddenly a large gap appeared in the white human wall, and Keevan had his first sight of the eggs. There didn't seem to be *any* left uncracked, and he could see the lucky boys standing beside wobble-legged dragons. He could hear the unmistakable plaintive crooning of hatchlings and their squawks of protest as they fell awkwardly in the sand.

Suddenly he wished that he hadn't left his bed, that he had stayed away from the Hatching Ground. Now everyone would see his ignominious failure. He scrambled now as desperately to reach the shadowy walls of the Hatching Ground as he had struggled to cross the bowl. He mustn't be seen.

He didn't notice, therefore, that the shifting group of boys remaining had begun to drift in his direction. The hard pace he had set himself and his cruel disappointment took their double toll of Keevan. He tripped and collapsed sobbing to the warm sands. He didn't see the consternation in the watching weyrfolk above the Hatching Ground, nor did he hear the excited whispers

77

of speculation. He didn't know that the weyrleader and weyrwoman had dropped to the arena and were making their way toward the knot of boys slowly moving in the direction of the archway.

"Never seen anything like it," the weyrleader was saying. "Only thirty-nine riders chosen. And the bronze trying to leave the Hatching Ground without making Impression!"

"A case in point of what I said last night," the weyrwoman replied, "where a hatchling makes no choice because the right boy isn't there."

"There's only Beterli and K'last's young one missing. And there's a full wing of boys to choose from. . . ."

"None acceptable, apparently. Where is the creature going? He's not heading for the entrance after all. Oh, what have we there, in the shadows?"

Keevan heard with dismay the sound of voices nearing him. He tried to burrow into the sand. The mere thought of the way he would be teased and taunted now was unbearable.

Don't worry! Please don't worry! The thought was urgent, but not his own.

Someone kicked sand over Keevan and butted roughly against him.

"Go away. Leave me alone!" he cried.

Why? was the injured-sounding question inserted into his mind. There was no voice, no tone, but the question was there, perfectly clear, in his head.

Incredulous, Keevan lifted his head and stared into the glowing jeweled eyes of a small bronze dragon. His wings were wet; the tips hung drooping to the sand. And he sagged in the middle on his unsteady legs, although he was making a great effort to keep erect.

Keevan dragged himself to his knees, oblivious to the

pain of his leg. He wasn't even aware that he was ringed by the boys passed over, while thirty-one pairs of resentful eyes watched him Impress the dragon. The weyrleaders looked on, amused and surprised at the draconic choice, which could not be forced. Could not be questioned. Could not be changed.

Why? asked the dragon again. *Don't you like me?* His eyes whirled with anxiety, and his tone was so piteous that Keevan staggered forward and threw his arms around the dragon's neck, stroking his eye ridges, patting the damp, soft hide, opening the fragile-looking wings to dry them, and assuring the hatchling wordlessly over and over again that he was the most perfect, most beautiful, most beloved dragon in the entire weyr, in all the weyrs of Pern.

"What's his name, K'van?" asked Lessa, smiling warmly at the new dragonrider. K'van stared up at her for a long moment. Lessa would know as soon as he did. Lessa was the only person who could "receive" from all dragons, not only her own Ramoth. Then he gave her a radiant smile, recognizing the traditional shortening of his name that raised him forever to the rank of dragonrider.

My name is Heath, thought the dragon mildly and hiccuped in sudden urgency: *I'm hungry.*

"Dragons are born hungry," said Lessa, laughing. "F'lar, give the boy a hand. He can barely manage his own legs, much less a dragon's."

K'van remembered his stick and drew himself up. "We'll be just fine, thank you."

"You may be the smallest dragonrider ever, young K'van, but you're the bravest," said F'lar.

And Heath agreed! Pride and joy so leaped in both chests that K'van wondered if his heart would burst

79

right out of his body. He looped an arm around Heath's neck and the pair—the smallest dragonboy and the hatchling who wouldn't choose anybody else—walked out of the Hatching Ground together forever.

5

The
Large Ant

by
Howard Fast

There have been all kinds of notions and guesses as to how it would end. One held that sooner or later there would be too many people; another that we would do each other in, and the atom bomb made that a very good likelihood. All sorts of notions, except the simple fact that we were what we were. We could find a way to feed any number of people and perhaps even a way to avoid wiping each other out with the bomb. Those things we are very good at, but we have never been any good at changing ourselves or the way we behave.

I know. I am not a bad man or a cruel man; quite to the contrary, I am an ordinary, humane person. I love my wife and my children, and I get along with my neighbors. I am like a great many other men. I do the things they would do and just as thoughtlessly. There it is in a nutshell.

I am also a writer, and I told Lieberman, the curator, and Fitzgerald, the government man, that I would like to write down the story. They shrugged their shoulders. "Go ahead," they said, "because it won't make one bit of difference."

"You don't think it would alarm people?"

"How can it alarm anyone when nobody will believe it?"

"If I could have a photograph or two."

"Oh, no," they said then. "No photographs."

"What kind of sense does that make?" I asked them. "You are willing to let me write the story—why not the photographs so that people could believe me?"

"They still won't believe you. They will just say you faked the photographs, but no one will believe you. It will make for more confusion, and if we have a chance of getting out of this, confusion won't help."

"What will help?"

They weren't ready to say that, because they didn't know.

So here is what happened to me, in a very straightforward and ordinary manner.

Every summer, sometime in August, four good friends of mine and I go for a week's fishing on the St. Regis chain of lakes in the Adirondacks. We rent the same shack each summer; we drift around in canoes, and sometimes we catch a few bass. The fishing isn't very good, but we play cards well together, and we cook out and generally relax. This summer past, I had some things to do that couldn't be put off. I arrived three days late, and the weather was so warm and even and beguiling that I decided to stay on by myself for a day or two after the others left. There was a small flat lawn in front of the shack, and I made up my mind to spend at least three or four hours at short putts. That was how I happened to have the putting iron next to my bed.

The first day I was alone, I opened a can of beans and a can of beer for my supper. Then I lay down in my bed with *Life on the Mississippi*, a pack of cigarettes, and an eight-ounce chocolate bar. There was nothing I had to do, no telephone, no demands, and no newspapers. At that moment, I was about as contented as any man can be in these nervous times.

It was still light outside, and enough light came in through the window above my head for me to read by. I was just reaching for a fresh cigarette, when I looked up and saw it on the foot of my bed. The edge of my hand was touching the golf club, and with a single motion I swept the club over and down, struck it a savage and accurate blow, and killed it. That was what I referred to before. Whatever kind of a man I am, I react as a man does. I think that any man, black, white, or yellow, in China, Africa, or Russia, would have done the same thing.

First I found that I was sweating all over, and then I knew I was going to be sick. I went outside to vomit, recalling that this hadn't happened to me since 1943, on my way to Europe on a tub of a Liberty ship. Then I felt better and was able to go back into the shack and look at it. It was quite dead, but I had already made up my mind that I was not going to sleep alone in this shack.

I couldn't bear to touch it with my bare hands. With a piece of brown paper, I picked it up and dropped it into my fishing creel. That, I put into the trunk case of my car, along with what luggage I carried. Then I closed the door of the shack, got into my car and drove back to New York. I stopped once along the road, just before I reached the thruway, to nap in the car for a little over an hour. It was almost dawn when I reached the city; and I had shaved, had a hot bath, and changed my clothes before my wife awoke.

During breakfast, I explained that I was never much of a hand at the solitary business, and since she knew

84

that, and since driving alone all night was by no means an extraordinary procedure for me, she didn't press me with any questions. I had two eggs, coffee, and a cigarette. Then I went into my study, lighted another cigarette, and contemplated my fishing creel, which sat upon my desk.

My wife looked in, saw the creel, remarked that it had too ripe a smell, and asked me to remove it to the basement.

"I'm going to dress," she said. The kids were still at camp. "I have a date with Ann for lunch—I had no idea you were coming back. Shall I break it?"

"No, please don't. I can find things to do that have to be done."

Then I sat and smoked some more, and finally I called the museum, and asked who the curator of insects was. They told me his name was Bertram Lieberman, and I asked to talk to him. He had a pleasant voice. I told him that my name was Morgan, and that I was a writer, and he politely indicated that he had seen my name and read something that I had written. That is formal procedure when a writer introduces himself to a thoughtful person.

I asked Lieberman if I could see him, and he said that he had a busy morning ahead of him. Could it be tomorrow?

"I am afraid it has to be now," I said firmly.

"Oh? Some information you require."

"No. I have a specimen for you."

"Oh?" The "oh" was a cultivated, neutral interval. It asked and answered and said nothing. You have to develop that particular "oh."

"Yes. I think you will be interested."

"An insect?" he asked mildly.

"I think so."

85

"Oh? Large?"

"Quite large," I told him.

"Eleven o'clock? Can you be here then? On the main floor, to the right, as you enter."

"I'll be there," I said.

"One thing—dead?"

"Yes, it's dead."

"Oh?" again. "I'll be happy to see you at eleven o'clock, Mr. Morgan."

My wife was dressed now. She opened the door to my study and said firmly, "Do get rid of that fishing creel. It smells."

"Yes, darling. I'll get rid of it."

"I should think you'd want to take a nap after driving all night."

"Funny, but I'm not sleepy," I said. "I think I'll drop around to the museum."

My wife said that was what she liked about me, that I never tired of places like museums, police courts, and third-rate nightclubs.

Anyway, aside from a racetrack, a museum is the most interesting and unexpected place in the world. It was unexpected to have two other men waiting for me, along with Dr. Lieberman, in his office. Lieberman was a skinny, sharp-faced man of about sixty. The government man, Fitzgerald, was small, dark-eyed, and wore gold-rimmed glasses. He was very alert, but he never told me what part of the government he represented. He just said "we," and it meant the government. Hopper, the third man, was comfortable-looking, pudgy, and genial. He was a United States senator with an interest in entomology, although before this morning I would have taken better than even money that such a thing not only wasn't, but could not be.

The room was large and square and plainly furnished, with shelves and cupboards on all walls.

We shook hands, and then Lieberman asked me, nodding at the creel, "Is that it?"

"That's it."

"May I?"

"Go ahead," I told him. "It's nothing that I want to stuff for the parlor. I'm making you a gift of it."

"Thank you, Mr. Morgan," he said, and he opened the creel and looked inside. Then he straightened up, and the other two men looked at him inquiringly.

He nodded. "Yes."

The senator closed his eyes for a long moment. Fitzgerald took off his glasses and wiped then industriously. Lieberman spread a piece of plastic on his desk, and then lifted the thing out of my creel and laid it on the plastic. The two men didn't move. They just sat where they were and looked at it.

"What do you think it is, Mr. Morgan?" Lieberman asked me.

"I thought that was your department."

"Yes, of course. I only wanted your impression."

"An ant. That's my impression. It's the first time I saw an ant fourteen, fifteen inches long. I hope it's the last."

"An understandable wish," Lieberman nodded.

Fitzgerald said to me, "May I ask how you killed it, Mr. Morgan?"

"With an iron. A golf club, I mean. I was doing a little fishing with some friends up at St. Regis in the Adirondacks, and I brought the iron for my short shots. They're the worst part of my game, and when my friends left, I intended to stay on at our shack and do four or five hours of short putts. You see—"

"There's no need to explain," Hopper smiled, a trace of sadness on his face. "Some of our very best golfers have the same trouble."

"I was lying in bed, reading, and I saw it at the foot of my bed. I had the club—"

"I understand," Fitzgerald nodded.

"You avoid looking at it," Hopper said.

"It turns my stomach."

"Yes—yes, I suppose so."

Lieberman said, "Would you mind telling us why you killed it, Mr. Morgan?"

"Why?"

"Yes—why?"

"I don't understand you," I said. "I don't know what you're driving at."

"Sit down, please, Mr. Morgan," Hopper nodded. "Try to relax. I'm sure this has been very trying."

"I still haven't slept. I want a chance to dream before I say how trying."

"We are not trying to upset you, Mr. Morgan," Lieberman said. "We do feel, however, that certain aspects of this are very important. That is why I am asking you why you killed it. You must have had a reason. Did it seem about to attack you?"

"No."

"Or make any sudden motion toward you?"

"No. It was just there."

"Then why?"

"This is to no purpose," Fitzgerald put in. "We know why he killed it."

"Do you?"

"The answer is very simple, Mr. Morgan. You killed it because you are a human being."

"Oh?"

"Yes. Do you understand?"

"No, I don't."

"Then why did you kill it?" Hopper put in.

"I was scared to death. I still am, to tell the truth."

88

Lieberman said, "You are an intelligent man, Mr. Morgan. Let me show you something." He then opened the doors of one of the wall cupboards, and there eight jars of formaldehyde and in each jar a specimen like mine—and in each case mutilated by the violence of its death. I said nothing. I just stared.

Lieberman closed the cupboard doors. "All in five days," he shrugged.

"A new race of ants," I whispered stupidly.

"No. They're not ants. Come here!" He motioned me to the desk and the other two joined me. Lieberman took a set of dissecting instruments out of his drawer, used one to turn the thing over, and then pointed to the underpart of what would be the thorax in an insect.

"That looks like part of him, doesn't it, Mr. Morgan?"

"Yes, it does."

Using two of the tools, he found a fissure and pried the bottom apart. It came open like the belly of a bomber; it was a pocket, a pouch, a receptacle that the thing wore, and in it were four beautiful little tools or instruments or weapons, each about an inch and a half long. They were beautiful the way any object of functional purpose and loving creation is beautiful—the way the creature itself would have been beautiful, had it not been an insect and myself a man. Using tweezers, Lieberman took each instrument off the brackets that held it, offering each to me. And I took each one, felt it, examined it, and then put it down.

I had to look at the ant now, and I realized that I had not truly looked at it before. We don't look carefully at a thing that is horrible or repugnant to us. You can't look at anything through a screen of hatred. But now the hatred and the fear were dilute, and as I looked, I realized it was not an ant although like an ant. It was nothing that I had ever seen or dreamed of.

All three men were watching me, and suddenly I was on the defensive. "I didn't know! What do you expect when you see an insect that size?"

Lieberman nodded.

"What in the name of God is it?"

From his desk, Lieberman produced a bottle and four small glasses. He poured and we drank it neat. I would not have expected him to keep good Scotch in his desk.

"We don't know," Hopper said. "We don't know what it is."

Lieberman pointed to the broken skull from which a white substance oozed. "Brain material—a great deal of it."

"It could be a very intelligent creature," Hopper nodded.

Lieberman said, "It is an insect in developmental structure. We know very little about intelligence in our insects. It's not the same as what we call intelligence. It's a collective phenomenon—as if you were to think of the component parts of our bodies. Each part is alive, but the intelligence is a result of the whole. If that same pattern were to extend to creatures like this one—"

I broke the silence. They were content to stand there and stare at it.

"Suppose it were?"

"What?"

"The kind of collective intelligence you were talking about."

"Oh? Well, I couldn't say. It would be something beyond our wildest dreams. To us—well, what we are to an ordinary ant."

"I don't believe that," I said shortly; and Fitzgerald, the government man, told me quietly, "Neither do we. We guess."

"If it's that intelligent, why didn't it use one of those weapons on me?"

"Would that be a mark of intelligence?" Hopper asked mildly.

"Perhaps none of these are weapons," Lieberman said.

"Don't you know? Didn't the others carry instruments?"

"They did," Fitzgerald said shortly.

"Why? What were they?"

"We don't know," Lieberman said.

"But you can find out. We have scientists, engineers —good God, this is an age of fantastic instruments. Have them taken apart!"

"We have."

"Then what have you found out?"

"Nothing."

"Do you mean to tell me," I said, "that you can find out nothing about these instruments—what they are, how they work, what their purpose is?"

"Exactly," Hopper nodded. "Nothing, Mr. Morgan. They are meaningless to the finest engineers and technicians in the United States. You know the old story— suppose you gave a radio to Aristotle. What would he do with it? Where would he find power? And what would he receive with no one to send? It is not that these instruments are complex. They are actually very simple. We simply have no idea of what they can or should do."

"But they must be a weapon of some kind."

"Why?" Lieberman demanded. "Look at yourself, Mr. Morgan—a cultured and intelligent man, yet you cannot conceive of a mentality that does not include weapons as a prime necessity. Yet a weapon is an unusual thing, Mr. Morgan. An instrument of murder.

91

We don't think that way, because the weapon has become the symbol of the world we inhabit. Is that civilized, Mr. Morgan? Or are the weapon and civilization in the ultimate sense incompatible? Can you imagine a mentality to which the concept of murder is impossible —or let me say absent? We see everything through our own subjectivity. Why shouldn't some other—this creature, for example—see the process of mentation out of his subjectivity? So he approaches a creature of our world—and he is slain. Why? What explanation? Tell me, Mr. Morgan, what conceivable explanation could we offer a wholly rational creature for this?" pointing to the thing on his desk. "I am asking you the question most seriously. What explanation?"

"An accident?" I muttered.

"And the eight jars in my cupboard? Eight accidents?"

"I think, Dr. Lieberman," Fitzgerald said, "that you can go a little too far in that direction."

"Yes, you would think so. It's a part of your own background. Mine is as a scientist. As a scientist, I try to be rational when I can. The creation of a structure of good and evil, or what we call morality and ethics, is a function of intelligence—and unquestionably the ultimate evil may be the destruction of conscious intelligence. That is why, so long ago, we at least recognized the injunction, 'thou shalt not kill!' even if we never gave more than lip service to it. But to a collective intelligence, such as this might be a part of, the concept of murder would be monstrous beyond the power of thought."

I sat down and lighted a cigarette. My hands were trembling. Hopper apologized. "We have been rather rough with you, Mr. Morgan. But over the past days, eight other people have done just what you did. We are caught in the trap of being what we are."

"But tell me—where do these things come from?"

"It almost doesn't matter where they come from," Hopper said hopelessly. "Perhaps from another planet —perhaps from inside this one—or the moon or Mars. That doesn't matter. Fitzgerald thinks they come from a smaller planet, because their movements are apparently slow on earth. But Dr. Lieberman thinks that they move slowly because they have not discovered the need to move quickly. Meanwhile, they have the problem of murder and what to do with it. Heaven knows how many of them have died in other places—Africa, Asia, Europe."

"Then why don't you publicize this? Put a stop to it before it's too late!"

"We've thought of that," Fitzgerald nodded. "What then—panic, hysteria, charges that this is the result of the atom bomb? We can't change. We are what we are."

"They may go away," I said.

"Yes, they may," Lieberman nodded. "But if they are without the curse of murder, they may also be without the curse of fear. They may be social in the highest sense. What does society do with a murderer?"

"There are societies that put him to death—and there are other societies that recognize his sickness and lock him away, where he can kill no more," Hopper said. "Of course, when a whole world is on trial, that's another matter. We have atom bombs now and other things, and we are reaching out to the stars—"

"I'm inclined to think that they'll run," Fitzgerald put in. "They may just have that curse of fear, Doctor."

"They may," Lieberman admitted. "I hope so."

But the more I think of it the more it seems to me that fear and hatred are the two sides of the same coin.

I keep trying to think back, to re-create the moment when I saw it standing at the foot of my bed in the fishing shack. I keep trying to drag out of my memory a clear picture of what it looked like, whether behind that chitinous face and the two gently waving antennae there was any evidence of fear and anger. But the clearer the memory becomes, the more I seem to recall a certain wonderful dignity and repose. Not fear and not anger.

And more and more, as I go about my work, I get the feeling of what Hopper called "a world on trial." I have no sense of anger myself. Like a criminal who can no longer live with himself, I am content to be judged.

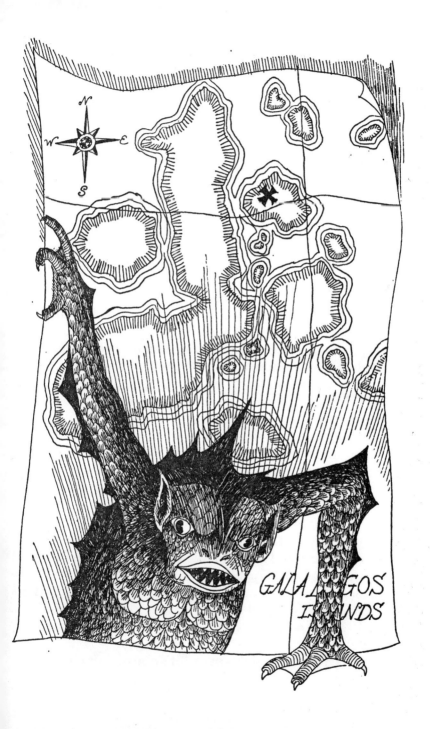

GALAPAGOS
ISLANDS

6

Dead Man's Chest

by
L. Sprague de Camp

Our son, Stephen, who had a summer job, arrived at Ocean Bay to spend a weekend with his old folks. Stephen was full of a plan that he and his friend Hank had dreamed up, to hunt for pirate treasure with a World War II mine detector on an island off the Jersey coast. A local tradition claimed that Captain Charles Vane had once put in there to bury his hoard.

Stephen told me about it while we labored through a round of miniature golf, into which he had coaxed me. Tennis is my game, although as a banker I have to play golf in the way of business. But Stephen is too slow and dreamy ever to make a tennis player.

The miniature course had fancy decorations. There were models of space rockets, grotesque animals like dinosaurs, and mythical monsters. One was a life-sized statue of a fish-man such as those my friend in Providence used to write about. It had fins running down its back and webbed hands and feet like those of a duck. It stood on a revolving turntable. I asked the ticket taker about it.

"I dunno," said this man. "It's one of them things that

crazy artist who designed this place put in. Said he'd seen one alive once, but it was probably a case of the d.t.'s. He's dead now."

We finished our round as Stephen wound up his account of the treasure-hunting plan. He looked at me apprehensively.

"I suppose," he said, "you'll tell me it couldn't possibly work, for some reason we never thought of."

"I don't want to spoil your fun," I said. "If you'd prefer, I won't say a word."

"No, go ahead, Dad. I'd rather have the bad news now than later, after we'd wasted our time."

"Okay. As I understand it, the routine on a pirate ship was, as soon as possible after taking a prize, to hold the share-out. This was done, not by the captain, but by the quartermaster, normally a pirate too old for pike-and-cutlass work but trusted by the crew. The division was equal, except that the captain might get a double share and the other ship's officers—the doctor, the gunner, and so on—might get one and a half shares, according to the ship's articles. Anyone who held back loot was liable to be hanged or at least keelhauled.

"You see, the captain didn't get all that rich from a capture. When the ship got back to its base, the pirates spent their shares in one grand bust. Rarely did enough loot accumulate in the hands of any one man to be worth burying. Moreover, I thought the pirate Vane stuck pretty close to the Caribbean."

Poor Stephen's mouth turned down, as it always did when I shot down one of his wild ideas. The year before, he and Hank had talked of going to the Galápagos Islands to grow copra. Somehow that sounded glamorous. I had to explain that, first, those islands did not produce copra; second, that copra was nothing but dried coconut meat, which stank in the process of drying and was eventually turned into shampoo oil or fed to the hogs in Iowa.

As things turned out, Stephen had a chance both to see the Galápagos Islands and to hunt for treasure much sooner than either of us expected.

The following summer, my boss, Esau Drexel, took off in his yacht for one of his expeditions in marine biology. Before he left, he said, "Willy, I can't take you on the whole cruise, because somebody has to run the trust company. But we're going to the Galápagos. Why don't you take Denise and the kids, fly to Guayaquil and Baltra, and meet me there? We can make a tour of the islands. It'll be a great experience, and you can be back in ten or twelve days. McGill can handle the business while you're gone."

It did not take much persuasion. Of my family, only Héloise, our undergraduate daughter, balked. She said her summer job was too important, she had promised her employers, and so on. I suspected that she did not want to go too far from the young man she was in love with. Stephen, who had just graduated from high school, was enthusiastic.

An airplane put Mr. and Mrs. Wilson Newbury, with son, Stephen, and daughter Priscille, down on the island of Baltra, where Drexel's *Amphitrite* was moored to the pier. The two little ships that took tourists around the islands were both out, so the *Amphitrite* had plenty of room.

Drexel, looking very pukka sahib in shorts and bush jacket, with his white moustache and sunburned nose, greeted us with his usual roar. With him was his wife, a little gray-haired woman who seldom got a chance to say much. There was another man, small, tanned, and white-haired, whom I had not met.

"This is Ronald Tudor," said Drexel. "Ronnie, meet Denise and Willy Newbury. Willy's the one who keeps the Harrison Trust from going broke while I'm away from the helm. Willy, Ronnie's the man who recovered the loot from the *Santa Catalina,* off Melbourne."

"Melbourne, Australia?" I asked.

"No, no, Melbourne, Florida. She was one of the treasure fleet wrecked there in 1715."

"Oh," I said. "Is that your regular business, Mr. Tudor?"

"Wouldn't ever call that kind of business regular," replied the little oldster with a sly grin. He had a quick, explosive way of speaking. "I do work at it off and on. Right now—but better wait till we shove off."

"You mean," said Priscille, "you're going to find some treasure in these islands, Mr. Tudor?"

"You'll see, young lady. Since we're not sailing till tomorrow morning, how about a swim?"

We swam from the nearby beach, where the hulk of a World War II landing craft lay upside down and rusting to pieces. The children had fun chasing ghost crabs. These, when cut off from their burrows, scuttled into the water and buried themselves out of sight.

Back at the *Amphitrite,* we met the Ecuadorian pilot, Flavio Ortega, as he came aboard. Flavio was a short, broad, copper-colored man with flat Mongoloid features. Although he must have been at least three-quarters Indian, he had the Hispanic bonhomie. When I tried my stumbling Castilian on him, he cried, "But, your accent is better than mine! *¡Usted habla como un caballero español!*"

He was a flatterer, of course, but one of life's lessons is that flattery will get you everywhere.

While we sat on the fantail swapping news before dinner, Esau Drexel explained. "The waters around these islands have got more rocks in them than the Democrats have in their heads. So we've got to have a local man to keep us from running into them."

"Well," I said, "how about Ronnie's great secret?"

When Tudor looked doubtful, Drexel said, "You can trust him as far as you can trust anybody, Ronnie. He's worked for me for ten years."

"Okay," said Tudor. "Wait a minute."

He went out and came back with a folder containing sheets of paper. In a lowered voice, he warned, "Be careful. Don't let water from your glass drip on these. They're only photostats, but we need 'em."

I examined the sheets. They were reproductions of three pages from an old manuscript, written in a large, clear longhand. The English had many obsolete usages, which put the document back two or three centuries. The sheets read as follows:

and so departed y^t Iland.

On June ye 6th, Capt. Eaton anchored in a Cove on ye NW Side of ye Iland, ye which Mr. Cowley hath named ye Duke of York's Iland. This Cove, which Mr. Cowley calls Albany Bay, is sheltered by a small, rocky Iland over against it. This little Iland hath a rocky Pinnacle, like unto a pointing Finger. Mr. Dampier assured us, y^t Water was to be found on ye larger Ilands, like unto y^s One, even during ye long Drought of Summer. Whiles ye Men went ashoar to seek for Springs or Brooks, Capt. Eaton privily took me aside and said: Mr. Henderson, ye Time hath come to bury y^t which lies in ye Chest. Sith I know you for a true Man, I will y^t ye and I, alone, shall undertake y^s ticklish Task, saying

Nought to Any. But Captain, I said, be ye determined upon y^s Course? For by God's Blood, sir, it seems to me y^t ye Contents of ye Chest would, if used with Sense and Prudence, furnish us with a handsome Living back in England for ye Rest of our mortal Dayes. If we ever get home, said Capt. Eaton; but with y^s accursed Thing aboard, I doubt me we ever shall. A Curse lies upon it; witness our Failure to take ye Spanish Ship whilst she had 800,000 Pieces of Eight aboard; so y^t all we gat for our Trouble was a Load of Flower, a Mule for the President of Panama, a wooden Image of ye Virgin, and 8 Tuns of Quince Marmalade. Well, saith he, verily, our Men have a Plenty of Flower wherewith to make Bread and of Jam to eat thereon, but we had liefer have ye Money. The Men also be in Fear of what it may bring upon us and will be happy to see ye Last of it.

So we went ashoar in ye Pinnace with ye Chest. Capt. Eaton and I carried ye Chest inland from ye Shoar and thence up ye Slope towards ye SW to ye Top of ye Cliff, which overlooks ye Cove. At ye Tip of ye Point, which marks ye western Limit of ye Bay, we buried ye Chest, and not without much hard Labour, for it was heavy to bear and ye rocky Soil hard to dig withal. When we returned to ye Ship

"Where did this come from?" I asked.

"Picked up the originals at an auction in London," said Tudor. "They're in a safe at home, naturally."

"Well, what does it mean?"

"Lord, don't you see, man?" Tudor exploded. "It's as plain as the nose on your face. This Henderson must have been one of the officers of Captain Eaton's *Nicholas*—the boatswain or the gunner, maybe—which stopped here in June 1684."

"How do you know the year?"

"Because he mentions Dampier and Cowley, who were here with him in the *Batchelor's Delight* at that time. The buccaneer Ambrose Cowley gave the islands their first set of individual names, although the Spaniards later rechristened them, and then the Ecuadorians gave them a third set. Gets confusing. Cowley called his island the Duke of York's Island. Then Charles Second died, and the Duke of York became James Second, so the island became James. Spanish called it Santiago, and then the Ecuadorians decided on San Salvador."

"Santiago ought to please everybody, since it means 'Saint James,'" I said, "although I don't believe James the Second was very saintly."

"Most English-speakers still use James," said Tudor.

"Is this all there is to the manuscript?"

"That's all. Did some sleuthing—British Museum and such—to try to locate the rest, but no dice. Probably somebody used it to light a fire. Couldn't find any other record of Henderson, either. But this is the important part, so—"

"All right, assuming the document refers to the present James or Santiago Island, do you think you can find this chest from these scanty directions? I thought James was a large island."

"It is, but the directions are as plain as a Michelin guidebook. This bay is what we call Buccaneer Cove. All we have to do is land there and follow Henderson's directions. With a metal detector, it ought to be a breeze."

I thought. "One more thing, Ronnie. The paper doesn't say what was *in* the chest. How do you know it's worth going after?"

"It wasn't money, or it would have been divided in the share-out. It was something of value, as you can tell by Henderson's comment. Evidently one single thing, not divisible. Must have been something of religious or supernatural significance, or the crew wouldn't have gotten spooked. My guess is, some fancy religious gew-gaw—a jeweled crown for a statue of the Virgin, or maybe a golden religious statuette, which the buccaneers stole from one of the Catholic churches along the coast. But what's the difference, we'll see when we dig it up. It's worth the chance."

Esau Drexel glanced over his shoulder and spoke in a low voice. "We need your help, Willy. I don't want to let the crew in on it, for obvious reasons, but this takes a bit of muscle. You remember how Henderson found the chest hefty to carry. Now, I'm too old and fat for hauling a couple of hundred pounds around rough country, and Ronnie's too old and small. There'll be some digging, too. But you're an athletic type, and your boy has pretty good muscles.

"Ronnie and I have agreed to go halves on whatever we find. If you'll come in with us, I'll give you half of my half, or a quarter of the total."

"Fair enough," I said. Drexel had his faults, but stinginess with his considerable wealth was not one of them.

At this time, the Galápagos Parque Nacional had been established only a few years, and things were not so tightly organized as they became later. Nowadays, I understand, the wardens would be down on you like a ton of gravel if you tried anything like treasure-hunting.

The next week we spent in cruising the southern islands. We saw the frigate birds and the blue-footed boobies on North Seymour. We were chased along the beach on Loberia by a big bull sea lion who thought we had designs on his harem. On Hood, we watched a pair of waved albatroses go through their courtship dance, waddling around each other and clattering their bills together. We gawked at swarms of marine iguanas, clinging to the black rocks and sneezing at us when we came close. We admired the flamingos in the muddy lagoon on Floreana.

On Plaza, Priscille, the strongest wildlife buff in the family, had the thrill of feeding some greenery to a big land iguana. That would not be allowed nowadays. On Santa Cruz (or Indefatigable) we visited the Charles Darwin Research Station. They told us of breeding tortoises in captivity, to reintroduce them on islands where they had been exterminated.

We dropped anchor in Buccaneer Cove on James, behind the islet with the rocky pinnacle of which Henderson had written. The four treasure hunters went ashore in the launch, leaving young Priscille furious at not being taken along. Denise was more philosophical.

"Have yourself the fun, my old," she said. "For me, to sit on a cactus once a trip is enough."

We left Flavio Ortega in charge of the boat, having told him we were looking for a brass marker plate left by Admiral de Torres in 1793.

"Be careful, gentlemen," he said. "There is said to be a—how do you say—*una maldición?*"

"A curse?" I said.

"Yes, of course, a curse. They say there is a curse on this place, from all the bisits of the wicked pirates who preyed on us poor Esspanish peoples. Of course, that is just a superstition; but watch your steps. The ground is treacherous."

We headed inland. Stephen carried the shovels, and I the pick and the goosenecked wrecking bar. Tudor toted the metal detector and Drexel, the lunch.

The weight of my burdens increased alarmingly as we scrambled up the rocky wall that bounded the beach. Above this rise, the sloping ground was fairly smooth, but parts of it were a talus of dark-gray sand made from disintegrated lava. Our feet sank into it, and it tended to slip out from under us.

There was a scattering of low shrubs. Higher, the hillsides were covered with an open stand of the pale-gray palo santo, or holy-stick trees, leafless at this time of year. Even the parts of these volcanic islands with a plant cover have an unearthly aspect, like a lunar landscape.

A narrow ravine cut through the terrain on its way to the bay. We had to climb the bluff on the eastern side of this gulch, as our goal lay on the west side. The ravine was too wide to jump, and its sides were too steep to scramble down and up. So we had to hike inland for half a mile or so until we found a place narrow enough to hop across. Drexel and Tudor were both pretty red and winded by that time.

The day was hotter and brighter than most. Although right on the equator, the Galápagos Islands (or Islas Encantadas or Archipiélago de Colón) are usually rather cool, because of the cold Humboldt Current and the frequent overcasts of the doldrum belt. I smeared suntan oil on my nose.

I could not help thinking of Ortega's curse. Most of my friends consider me a paragon of cold rationality and common sense, never fooled by mummeries and superstitions. In my business, that is a useful reputation. But still, funny things have happened to me. . . .

On the western side of the ravine, we hiked back down the slope. Then we cut across toward the tip of the western point, keeping at more or less the same altitude. When we neared the apex, we stopped to let Tudor set up the metal detector.

As he thumbed the switch, the instrument gave out a faint hum. Tudor began to quarter the area. He moved slowly, a step at a time, swinging the head of the detector back and forth as if he were sweeping or vacuum-cleaning.

Drexel, Stephen, and I sat on the slope and ate our lunch. A handbill given us at Baltra warned us not to leave any litter. Nowadays they are even tougher about it.

The detector continued its hum, getting louder or softer as Tudor came nearer or went farther away. It made me nervous to see him close to the tip of the point. The surface on which he was working was fairly steep, so that walking took an effort of balance. If you fell down and rolled or slid, you might have trouble stopping yourself. This slope continued down to the top of the cliff, which here was a forty-foot vertical drop into the green Pacific.

At last, when Tudor was twenty-five or thirty feet from the edge, the hum of the instrument changed to a warble. Tudor stood a long time, swinging the detector.

"Here y'are," he said. "I'll eat my lunch while you fellas dig."

Since Stephen and I were the muscle men, we fell to. There was no sound but the faint sigh of the breeze, the scrape of the shovels, and the bark of a distant sea lion. Once Stephen, stopping to wipe the sweat from his face, cried, "Hey, Dad, look!"

He pointed to the dorsal fin of a shark, which lazily cut the water beyond the cliff. We watched it out of sight and resumed our digging. Having finished his lunch, Tudor came forward to wave his detector over the pit we had dug. The warble was loud and clear.

We began getting into hardpan, so that we had to take the pick to loosen stones of increasing size. Then the pick struck something that did not sound like another stone.

"Hey!" said Drexel.

We soon uncovered the top of a chest, the size of an old-fashioned steamer trunk and much distressed by age. Drexel, Tudor, and Stephen chattered excitedly. I kept quiet, a dim foreboding having taken hold of me. Somehow the conviction formed in my mind that, if the chest were opened, one of us would die.

Tudor was nothing to me; I distrust adventurer types. I should be sorry to lose Drexel, a friend as well as a boss. But the thought crossed my mind that I might succeed him as president of the trust company. I was ashamed of the thought, but there it was. For myself, I was willing to take chances. But that anything should happen to Stephen was unbearable.

I wanted to shout: Stop, leave that thing alone! Or, at least, let me send Stephen back to the ship before you open it. But what argument could I offer? It was nothing but an irrational feeling—the kind of premonition we get from time to time but remember only on the rare occasions when it is fulfilled by the event. I had no evidence.

"Tired, Willy?" Drexel asked. "Here, give me that shovel!"

He grabbed the implement and began digging in his turn, grunting and blowing like a walrus. Soon he and Stephen had the chest excavated down below the lower edge of the lid.

The chest had a locked iron clasp, but this was a mass

of rust. The wood of the chest was so rotten that, at the first pry with the wrecking bar, the lock tore out of the wood. Stephen burst into song:

> "Fifteen men on the dead man's chest—
> Yo-ho-ho, and a bottle of rum!
> Drink and the devil had done for the rest—
> Yo-ho-ho, and a—"

He broke off as Drexel and Tudor lifted the lid with a screech of ancient hinges.

"Lord!" said Ronald Tudor. "What's this?"

In the chest, face up, lay a fish-man like that of which a statue stood in the miniature golf course at Ocean Bay. The thing had been bound with leather thongs in a doubled-up position, with its knees against its chest. Its eyes were covered by a pair of large gold coins.

"Some kind of sea monster," Drexel breathed. "Oh, boy, if I can only get it as a specimen for the museum."

Tudor, eyes agleam, shot out two skinny hands and snatched the coins. He jerked away with a startled yelp. "The cursed thing's alive!"

The fish-man's bulging eyes opened. For one breath it lay in its coffin, regarding us with a walleyed stare. Then its limbs moved into jerky action. The leather thongs, brittle with age, snapped like grass stems.

The fish-man's webbed, three-fingered hands gripped the sides of the chest. It heaved itself into a sitting position and stood up. It started to climb out of the excavation.

"Good Lord!" cried Tudor.

The fish-man was climbing out on the side toward the sea, which happened to be the side on which Tudor stood. Tudor, apparently thinking himself attacked, shoved the coins into his pants pocket, snatched up a

108

shovel, and swung it at the fish-man.

The blade of the shovel thudded against the fish-man's scaly shoulder. The fish-man opened its mouth, showing a row of long, sharp, fish-catching teeth. It gave a hiss, like the noise a Galápagos tortoise makes when it withdraws into its shell.

"Don't—I mean—" cried Drexel.

As Tudor swung the shovel back for another blow, the fish-man moved stiffly toward him, fangs bared, arms and webbed hands spread. Tudor stumbled back, staggering and slipping in the loose, sloping soil. The two moved toward the cliff, Tudor dodging from side to side and threatening the fish-man with his shovel.

"Watch out!" yelled Drexel and I together.

Tudor backed off the cliff and vanished. The monster dove after him. Two splashes came up, in quick succession, from below.

When we reached the top of the cliff, Tudor's body was lying awash below us. We caught a glimpse of the fish-man, flapping swiftly along like a sea lion just below the surface and heading for deep water. In a few seconds, it was gone.

"We've got to see if Ronnie's alive," said Drexel.

"Stevie," I said, "run back to the top of the little cliff just this side of the ravine. Call down to Flavio, telling him to bring the boat. Don't mention the monster—"

"Aw, Dad, I can get down that little cliff." Stephen was gone before I could argue. He slithered down the cliff like a marine iguana and leaped the last ten feet to sprawl on the beach. In a minute he was in the launch, which soon buzzed around to the place where Tudor had fallen.

Stephen and Ortega got Tudor into the boat, but he was already dead. He had been dashed against a point of rock in his fall.

"Maybe," said Ortega, "there is a evil esspell on this place after all."

"Well," said Drexel later, "at least we know now what Captain Eaton meant by 'ye accursed Thing.'"

We sailed back to Baltra and arranged for the local burial of Ronald Tudor.

"He was kind of a con man," said Drexel, "but an interesting one. Let's not put anything in our report to the local authorities about the monster. We don't have a specimen to show, and the Ecuadorians might think we had murdered poor Ronnie and were trying to cover it up with a wild yarn."

So we said only that our companion had met death by misadventure. While I had not much liked the man, his death cast a pall on our vacation. Instead of rounding out our tour by visiting Tower, Isabela, and Fernandina Islands, we cut it short. Drexel sailed for the Panama Canal, while the Newburys flew home. After we got back, it was as if Ronald Tudor and the fish-man had never existed.

But, although I have been back to Ocean Bay several times since, nobody has ever again inveigled me into playing a round at that miniature golf course. To have the revolving statue of a fish-man goggling at me while I was addressing the ball would give me the willies. No pun intended.

7

Socrates

by
John Christopher

I had closed the lab for the afternoon and was walking down toward the front gate, meaning to take a bus into town, when I heard the squeals from the direction of the caretaker's cottage. I'm fond of animals and hate to hear them in pain, so I walked through the gate into the cottage yard. What I saw horrified me.

Jennings, the caretaker, was holding a young puppy in his hand and beating its head against the stone wall. At his feet were three dead puppies, and as I came through the gate he tossed a fourth among them, and picked up the last squirming remnant of the litter. I called out sharply, "Jennings! What's going on?"

He turned to face me, still holding the puppy in his hand. He is a surly-looking fellow at best, but now he looked thunderous.

"What's it look like I'm doing?" he demanded. "Killing off a useless litter—that's what I'm doing."

He held the pup out for me to observe.

"Here," he went on, "have a look at this and you'll see why."

I looked closely. It was the queerest pup I had ever

seen. It had a dirty tan coat and abnormally thick legs. But it was the head that drew my attention. It must have been fully four times the size of any ordinary pup of its breed; so big that, although its neck was sturdy, the head seemed to dangle on it like an apple on a stalk.

"It's a queer one, all right," I admitted.

"Queer?" he exclaimed. "It's a monster, that's what it is." He looked at me angrily. "And I know the cause of it. I'm not a fool. There was a bit in the Sunday papers a couple of weeks back about it. It's them electrical X-ray machines you have up at the house. It said in the paper about X-rays being able to influence what's to be born and make monsters of them. And look at this for a litter of pedigree airedales; not one that would make even a respectable mongrel. Thirty quid the price of this litter at the very least."

"It's a pity," I said, "but I'm pretty sure the company won't accept responsibility. You must have let your bitch run loose beyond the inner gate, and there's no excuse for that. It's too bad you didn't see that bit in the Sunday paper a few weeks earlier; you might have kept her chained up more. You know you've been warned about going near the plant."

"Yes," he snarled, "I know what chance I've got of getting money out of those crooks. But at least I can get some pleasure out of braining this lot."

He prepared to swing the pup against the wall. It had been quiet while we were talking, but now it gave one low howl and opened large eyes in a way that seemed fantastically to suggest that it had been listening to our conversation, and knew its fate was sealed. I grabbed hold of Jennings' arm pretty roughly.

"Hold on," I said. "When did you say those pups were born?"

"This morning," he growled.

I said, "But its eyes are open. And look at the color! Have you ever seen an airedale with blue eyes before?"

He laughed unpleasantly. "Has anybody ever seen an airedale with a head like that before, or a coat like that? It's no more an airedale than I am. It's a cur. And I know how to deal with it."

The pup was whining to itself, as though realizing the futility of making louder noises. I pulled my wallet out.

"I'll give you a quid for it," I said.

He whistled. "You must be mad," he said. "But why should that worry me? It's yours for the money. Taking it now?"

"I can't," I said. "My landlady wouldn't let me. But I'll pay you ten bob a week if you will look after it till I can find it a place. Is it a deal?"

He put his hand out again. "In advance?"

I paid him.

"I'll look after it, guv'nor, even though it goes against the grain. At any rate it'll give Glory something to mother."

At least once a day, sometimes twice, I used to call in to see how the pup was getting along. It was progressing amazingly. At the end of the second week Jennings asked for an increase of 2/6d. in the charge for keeping it, and I had to agree. It had fed from the mother for less than a week, after which it had begun to eat its own food, and with a tremendous appetite.

Jennings scratched his unkempt head when he looked at it. "I don't know. I've never seen a dog like it. Glory didn't give it no lessons in eating or drinking. It just watched her from the corner and one day, when I brought fresh stuff down, it set on it like a wolf. It ain't natural."

Watching the pup eat, I was amazed myself. It

114

seemed to have more capacity for food than its mother, and you could almost see it putting on weight and size. And its cleverness! It was hardly more than a fortnight old when I surprised it carefully pawing the latch of the kennel door open to get at some food that Jennings had left outside while going out to open the gates. But even at that stage I don't think it was such superficial tricks that impressed me, so much as the way I would catch it watching Jennings and me as we leaned over the kennel fence discussing it. There was such an air of attentiveness about the way it sat, with one ear cocked, a puzzled frown on that broad-browed, most uncanine face.

Jennings said one day, "Thought of a name for him yet?"

"Yes," I said. "I'm going to call him Socrates."

"Socrates?" repeated Jennings. "Something to do with football?"

I smiled. "There was another great thinker with that name several thousand years ago. A Greek."

"Oh," Jennings said scornfully, "a Greek . . ."

One Friday evening I brought a friend down to see Socrates—a man who had made a study of dogs. Jennings wasn't in. This didn't surprise me because he habitually got drunk at least one evening a week and Friday was his favorite. I took my friend around to the kennels.

He didn't say anything when he saw the pup, which was now, after three weeks, the size of a large fox terrier. He examined it carefully, as though he were judging a prize winner at Cruft's. Then he put it down and turned to me.

"How old did you say this dog is?" he asked.

I told him.

He shook his head. "If it were anyone but you who

115

told me, I would call him a liar," he said. "Man, I've never seen anything like it. And that head . . . You say the rest of the litter were the same?"

"The bodies looked identical," I told him. "That's what impressed me. You are liable to get freak mutations round these new labs of ours—double-headed rats and that sort of thing—but five the same in one litter! That looked like a true mutation to me."

He said, "Mutations I'm a bit shaky about, but five alike in one litter look like a true breed to me. What a tragedy that fool killed them."

"He killed a goose that might have laid him some very golden eggs," I said. "Quite apart from the scientific importance of it—I should imagine a biologist would go crazy at the thought—a new mutated breed like this would have been worth a packet. Even this one dog might have all sorts of possibilities. Look!"

Socrates had pushed an old tin against the wall of the kennel and was using it in an attempt to scale the fence barring the way to the outer world. His paws scrabbled in vain a few inches from the top.

"Lord!" my friend said. "If it can do that after a month . . ."

We turned and left the kennels. As we came out, I collided with Jennings. He reeled drunkenly past us.

"Come to feed little Shocratesh," he said thickly.

I held his shoulder. "That's all right," I said. "We've seen to them."

When I dropped in the following day, I was surprised to see a huge, roughly painted sign hanging over the kennel door. It read: PRIVATE. NO ADMITTANCE.

I tried the door, but it was locked. I looked around. Jennings was watching me.

"Hello, Professor," he said. "Can't you read?"

I said, "Jennings, I've come for the pup. My friend is

116

going to look after him at his kennels."

Jennings grinned. "Sorry," he said, "the dog's not for sale."

"What do you mean?" I exclaimed. "I bought him four weeks ago. And I've been paying you for his keep."

"You got any writing that says that, Professor?" he asked. "You got a bill of sale?"

"Don't be ridiculous, Jennings," I said. "Open the door up."

"You even got any witnesses?" he asked. He came over to me confidentially.

"Look," he said, "you're a fair man. I heard you telling your friend last night that dog's a gold mine. You know I own him by rights. Here, I'm a fair man myself. Here's three pounds five; the money I've had from you in the last four weeks. You know he's my gold mine by rights. You wouldn't try to do a man like me. You know I paid five quid stud fee for that litter."

"It was a bargain," I said. "You were going to throw the pup at the wall—don't forget that. You wouldn't even know the dog was anything out of the ordinary now, except for listening to a private conversation last night." I found my wallet. "Here's ten pounds. That will make good the stud fee and a little extra profit for yourself into the bargain."

He shook his head. "I'm not selling, Professor. And I know my rights in the law. You've got no proof; I've got possession."

I said, "You idiot! What can you do with him? He will have to be examined by scientists, tested, trained. You don't know anything about it."

Jennings spat on the ground. "Scientists!" he exclaimed. "No, I'm not taking him to no scientists. I've got a bit of money saved up. I'm off away from here tomorrow. *I'll* do the training. And you watch the

117

theaters for the big billboards in a few months' time—
George Jennings and his Wonder Dog, Socrates! I'll be
up at the West End inside a year."

It was only three months later that I saw the name on
the bills outside the Empire Theater in Barcaster.
There had been no word from Jennings during that
time. As he had said he would, he had gone with the
dog, vanishing completely. Now he was back, and the
bill read as he had told me it would:

GEORGE JENNINGS
AND HIS WONDER DOG,
SOCRATES

I went in and bought a seat in the front row. There
were some knockabout comedians fooling together on
the stage, and after them a team of rather tired-looking
acrobats. Jennings was the third in appearance. He
strode on to a fanfare of trumpets, and behind him
loped Socrates.

He was bigger and his rough, tan coat was shaggier
than ever. His head was more in proportion to his body,
too, but it was still huge. He looked nearer to a St.
Bernard than any breed I could think of, but he was
very little like a St. Bernard. He was just Socrates, with
the same blazing blue eyes that had surprised me that
afternoon four months before.

Jennings had taught him tricks, all right. As they
reached the center of the stage, Socrates stood up on his
hind legs, waddled to the footlights, and saluted the
audience. He swung effortlessly from the trapezes the
acrobats had left, and spelled out words in reply to
Jennings' questions, pulling alphabet blocks forward
with his teeth. He went through all the repertoire that
trick dogs usually follow, capping them with an assur-

ance that made the audience watch in respectful silence. But when he left, walking stiffly off the stage, the ovation was tremendous. They came back half a dozen times for encores, Socrates saluting gravely each time the mob of hysterical humans before him. When they had left for the last time, I walked out too.

I bribed the doorman to let me know the name of Jennings' hotel. He wasn't staying with the rest of the music-hall people but by himself in the Grand. I walked over there late in the evening and had my name sent up. The small, grubby page boy came back in a few minutes.

"Mr. Jennings says you're to go right up," he told me and added the floor and room number.

I knocked and heard Jennings' voice answer, "Come in!"

He seemed more prosperous than the Jennings I had known, but there was the same shifty look about him. He was sitting in front of the fire wearing an expensive blue-and-gold dressing gown, and as I entered the room he poured himself whiskey from a decanter. I noticed that his hand shook slightly.

"Why," he said thickly, "if it isn't the professor! Always a pleasure to see old friends. Have a drink, Professor."

He helped me to whiskey.

"Here's to you, Professor," he said, "and to Socrates, the Wonder Dog!"

I said, "Can I see him?"

He grinned. "Any time you like. Socrates!"

A door pushed open and Socrates walked in, magnificent in his bearing and in the broad, intelligent face from which those blue eyes looked out. He advanced to Jennings' chair and dropped into immobility, head couched between powerful paws.

119

"You seen our show?" Jennings asked.

I nodded.

"Great, isn't it? But it's only the beginning. We're going to show them! Socrates, do the new trick."

Socrates jumped up and left the room, returning a moment later pulling a small wooden go-cart, gripping a rope attached to it in his teeth. I noticed that the cart had a primitive pedal arrangement near the front, fixed to the front wheels. Socrates suddenly leaped into the cart and, moving the pedals with his paws, propelled himself along the room. As he reached the wall the cart swerved, and I noticed that his tail worked a rudderlike arrangement for steering. He went the reverse length of the room and turned again, but this time failed to allow enough clearance. The cart hit the side wall, and Socrates toppled off.

Jennings rose to his feet in an instant. He snatched a whip from the wall and while Socrates cowered, thrashed him viciously, cursing him all the time for his failure.

I jumped forward and grappled with Jennings. At last I got the whip away from him, and he fell back exhausted in the chair and reached for the whiskey decanter.

I said angrily, "You madman! Is this how you train the dog?"

He looked up at me over his whiskey glass. "Yes," he said, "this is my way of training him! A dog's got to learn respect for his master. He doesn't understand anything but the whip. Socrates!"

He lifted his whip hand, and the dog cowered down.

"I've trained him," he went on. "He's going to be the finest performing dog in the world before I'm through."

I said, "Look, Jennings, I'm not a rich man, but I've

120

got friends who will advance me money. I'll get you a thousand pounds for Socrates."

He sneered. "So you want to cash in on the theaters, too?"

"I promise that if you sell Socrates to me, he will never be used for profit by anyone."

He laughed. "What the devil do I care what would happen to him if I sold him. But I'm not selling; not for a penny under £20,000. Why, the dog's a gold mine."

"You are determined about that?" I asked.

He got up again. "I'll get you the advance bills for our next engagement," he said. "Top billing already! Hang on; they're only next door."

He walked out unsteadily. I looked down to where Socrates lay, watching everything in the way that had fascinated me when he was a pup. I called to him softly, "Socrates."

He pricked up his ears. I felt crazy, but I had to do it. I whispered to him, "Socrates, follow me back as soon as you can get away. Here, take the scent from my coat."

I held my sleeve out to him, and he sniffed it. He wagged his huge, bushy tail slowly. Then Jennings was back with his billheads, and I made my excuses and left.

I walked back—a matter of two or three miles. The more I thought, the more insane did it seem that the dog could have heeded and understood my message. It had been an irrational impulse.

I had found new accommodations in the months since Jennings' disappearance, in a cottage with a friendly old couple. I had brought Tess, my own golden retriever, from home, and the couple adored her. She was sitting on the inside window ledge as I walked slowly up the garden path, and her barks brought old

Mrs. Dobby to the door to let me in. Tess came bouncing to meet me, and her silky paws were flung up toward my chest. I patted and stroked her into quietness and, after washing, settled down to a pleasant tea.

Two or three hours later, the Dobbys having gone to bed, I was sitting reading by the fire when I heard a voice at the door.

I called, "Who's there?"

This time it was a little more distinct, though still garbled, as though by a person with a faulty palate. I heard, "Socrates."

I threw the door open quickly. Socrates stood there, eyes gleaming, tail alert. I looked beyond him into the shadows.

"Who's brought you, old chap?" I asked.

Socrates looked up. His powerful jaws opened. I could see teeth gleaming whitely.

Socrates said, slurring the words, but intelligible, "Me. Can speak."

I brought him in, shelving my incredulity. As I sat in the Dobbys' cozy room in front of a glowing fire, it seemed more fantastic than ever. Half to myself, I said, "I can't believe it."

Socrates had sat down on the rug. "True, though," he said.

I asked, "Does Jennings know?"

Socrates replied, "No. Have told no one else. Would only make into tricks."

"But Jennings knows you can hear and understand things?"

"Yes. Could not hide. Jennings whips until I learn. Easier to learn at once."

His voice, a kind of low, articulate growling, became more readily understandable as I listened to it. After a few minutes it did not seem at all strange that I was sitting by the fire talking to a half-grown but large mongrel dog. He told me how he had practiced human speech by himself, forcing his throat to adapt itself to its complexities, succeeding through a long process of trial and error.

I said, in amazement, "But, Socrates, you are barely four months old!"

His brow wrinkled. "Yes. Strange. Everything goes so fast for me. Big . . . old . . ."

"Maturity," I supplied. "Of course there have been 'talking dogs' before, but they were just stunts, no real intelligence. Do you realize what a phenomenon you are, Socrates?"

The vast canine face seemed to smile. "How not realize?" he asked. "All other dogs—such fools. Why that, Professor?"

I told him of his birth. He seemed to grasp the idea of X-ray mutation very easily. I suppose one can always swallow the facts of one's own existence. He remembered very little of that first month of infancy. When I told him of the fate of the rest of his litter, he was saddened.

"Perhaps best not to know that," he said. "Sad to think I might have had brothers and sisters like me. Not to be always a trick dog."

"You don't need to be a trick dog, Socrates," I said. "Look, we'll go away. I've got friends who will help. You need never see Jennings again."

Socrates said, "No. Not possible. Jennings the master. I must go back."

"But he beats you! He may beat you for going out now."

"He will," Socrates said. "But worth it to come see you."

"Look, Socrates," I said. "Jennings isn't your master.

123

No free intelligence should be a slave to another. Your intelligence is much more advanced than Jennings'."

The big head shook. "For men, all right. Dogs different."

"But you aren't even Jennings' dog," I said. I told him the story of Jennings' trickery; how he had sold Socrates to me and then refused to acknowledge the sale. Socrates was not impressed.

"Always Jennings' dog," he said. "Not remember anything else. Must go back. You not dog—not understand."

I said halfheartedly, "We would have a fine time, Socrates. You could learn all sorts of things. And be free, completely free."

But I knew it was no use. Socrates, as he said, was still a dog, even though an intelligent one, and the thousands of years of instinctive slavery to a human master had not been quenched by the light that brought intelligence and reasoning to his brain.

He said, "Will come here to learn. Will get away often."

"And be beaten by Jennings every time you go back?"

Socrates shivered convulsively. "Yes," he said. "Worth it. Worth it to learn things. You teach?"

"I'll teach you anything I can, Socrates," I promised.

"Can mutate more dogs like me?"

I hated to say it. "No, Socrates. You were a fluke, an accident. X-rays make monsters; once in a million, million times, perhaps, something like you happens."

The bushy tail drooped disconsolately. The huge head rested a moment between his paws. Then he stood up, four-legged, an outcast.

"Must go now. Will come again soon."

I let him out and saw him lope away into the night.

I turned back into the warm, firelit room. I thought of Socrates, running back through the night to Jennings' whip, and I knew what anger and despair were.

Socrates came quite frequently after that. He would sit in front of me while I read to him from books. At first he wanted to be taught to read for himself, but the difficulty of turning pages with his clumsy paws discouraged him. I read to him from all the books he wanted.

His appetite was voracious, but lay chiefly along nontechnical lines, naturally enough, in view of the impossibility of his ever being able to do even the simplest manual experiments. Philosophy interested him, and I found my own education improving with Socrates'. He enjoyed poetry, too, and composed a few rough poems, which had the merit of a strange nonhuman approach. But he would not let me write them down; now I can remember only a few isolated lines.

His most intense interest was in an unexpected field. I mentioned casually one day some new development in psychical research, and his mind fastened on the subject immediately. He told me he could see all sorts of queer things which he knew humans could at best sense only vaguely. He spent nearly an hour one evening describing to me the movements of a strange spiral-shaped thing that, he said, was spinning around slowly in one corner of my room, now and then increasing and decreasing in size and making sudden jumps. I walked over to the place he indicated and put my hand through vacancy.

"Can hear it, too," Socrates said. "High, sweet noise."

"Some people have unusual senses and report similar things," I told him.

He made me read through every book I could find on

paranormal phenomena, in search of explanations of the oddities that surrounded him, but the authors annoyed him.

"So many fools," he said wearily, when we put down one book. "They did not see. They only wanted to. They thought they did."

The Dobbys were a little curious at my new habit of reading aloud in my room, and once I saw them glancing suspiciously at Socrates when he changed his speech into a growl as they came into the house from the garden. But they accepted his strange appearances and disappearances quite easily, and always made a fuss of him when he happened to turn up during my absence.

We did not always read. At times we would go out into the fields, and he and Tess would disappear in search of rabbits and birds and all the other things that fascinate dogs in the country. I would see them a field away, breasting the wind together. Socrates badly needed such outings. Jennings rarely took him out, and, as Socrates spent all the time he could filch from Jennings' training activities with me, he saw no other dogs and had no other exercise. Tess was very fond of him and sometimes whined when we shut her out from my room in order to read and talk undisturbed. I asked Socrates about her once.

He said, "Imagine all dogs intelligent; all men fools. You the only intelligent man. You talk to dogs, but you not like pretty women, even though they are fools?"

Then, for months, Socrates disappeared, and I learned that Jennings was touring the north of England, having a sensational success. I saw also the announcement that he was to return to Barcaster for a fortnight early in November. I waited patiently. On the morning before Jennings was due to open, Socrates returned.

He was looking as fit as ever physically, but mentally the tour had been a strain for him. In philosophy he had always inclined to defeatism, but it had been defeat with a sense of glory. He had reveled in Stapledon's works and drawn interesting comparisons between himself and Stapledon's wonder sheep dog. Now, however, there was a listlessness about him that made his defeatism a drab and unhappy thing. He would not read philosophy, but lay silent while I read poetry to him.

Jennings, I discovered, had steadily increased his bouts of drunkenness. Socrates told me that he had to carry the act by himself now. Jennings was generally too drunk to give even the most elementary instructions on the stage.

And, of course, with the drunkenness came the whippings. There were nasty scars on the dog's back. I treated them as well as I could; but increasingly I hated and dreaded the time when he would say, "Must go now," and I would see him lope off, tail low, to face Jennings' drunken fury.

I remonstrated with him again, begging him to come away with me, but it was beyond reason. The centuries of slavery could not be eradicated. He always went back to Jennings.

Then he came one afternoon. It had been raining for days, and he was wet through. He would not stay in front of the fire to dry. The rain was slackening a little. I took my raincoat, and, with Tess frisking beside us, we set out. We walked on in silence. Even Tess grew subdued.

At last, Socrates said, "Can't go on for long. Whipped me again last night. Felt something burn my mind. Almost tore his throat out. I will do it soon, and they will shoot me."

"They won't shoot you," I said. "You come to me. You will be all right. Come now, Socrates. Surely you don't want to go on serving Jennings when you know you may have to kill him?"

He shivered, and the raindrops ran off his shaggy back.

"Talking no good," he said. "I must go back. And if he whips me too much, I must kill him. I will be shot. Best that way."

We had reached the river. I paused on the bridge that spanned it a few inches above the swirling currents of the flood and looked out. The river was high after the rain, running even more swiftly than it usually did. Less than a quarter of a mile away was the fall, where the water cascaded over the brink into a raging turmoil below. I was looking at it abstractedly when I heard Jennings' voice.

He stood at the other end of the bridge. He was raging drunk.

He called, "So there you are! And that's what you've been up to—sneaking off to visit the professor. I thought I might catch you here."

He advanced menacingly up the bridge. "What you need, my lad, is a taste of the whip."

He was brandishing it as he walked. I waited until he had almost reached the place where Socrates was cowering on the boards, waiting for the blow, and then I charged him savagely. He fought for a moment, but I was sober and he was not. I caught one of his legs and twisted. He pulled viciously away, staggered, fell—and disappeared into the violently flowing river.

I saw his face appear a few yards down. He screamed and went under again. I turned to Socrates.

"It's all over," I said. "You are free. Come home, Socrates."

The head appeared again and screamed more faintly. Socrates stirred. He called to Jennings for the first and last time, "Master!"

Then he was over the bridge and swimming frantically toward the drowning man. I called after him, but he took no notice. I thought of jumping in myself, but I knew I could not last even to reach him. With Tess at my heels, I raced round the bank to the place where the water roared over the fall.

I saw them just as they reached the fall. Socrates had reached him and was gripping the coat in his teeth. He tried to make for the bank, but there was no chance. They were swept over the edge and into the fury below.

I watched for their reappearance for some time, but they did not come up.

They never came up.

I think sometimes of the things Socrates might have done if he had been given the chance. If only for those queer things he saw that we cannot see, his contribution to knowledge would have been tremendous. And when I think that he was less than a year old when he died, the lost possibilities awe and sadden me.

I cannot escape the conclusion that at his full maturity he would have outstripped all the specialists in the strange fields he might have chosen to work in.

There is just one thing that worries me still. His was a true mutation; the identical litter showed that. But was it a dominant one? Could the strength and vigor of his intelligence rise above the ordinary traits of an ordinary dog? It's a point that means a great deal.

Tess is going to have pups.

8

The
Horse Show

by
Catherine Crook de Camp

Otis J. Claymont, Jr., was a loser. For one thing, he was small for his age and an all-A student. For another, while he lived in a very horsey neighborhood, he did not own a horse. Worse yet, his father, instead of riding the monorail to his office three days a week, spent most of his time rocketing toward planets that did not even appear in the junior high galactic cosmography books. Although there wasn't anything really wrong with piloting an interplanetary freighter, well, it just was not the sort of thing that most of the men who lived in Montague Manor did for a living in the year 2015.

The kids at school teased O.J. constantly. Jim Painter, the biggest boy in the class, always called O.J. "Oh, 'tis Junior" or "Teacher's Shadow." Jim's friends followed their leader, all except pretty Betsy Drake, who liked everybody. She would tell the others to get off O.J.'s back, and once in a while she would even smile at him. O.J. blamed the teasing on his father's job, on his own oversized vocabulary, and on the braces on his teeth. He never guessed that his shyness made him seem cold and unfriendly. After a while, he began to feel cold and

132

unfriendly and had little or nothing to do with his class-mates.

Although O.J. did not love people, he loved horses. The kids used to say that he "talked horse" because whenever he leaned across a fence and called softly, even the youngest foal would come up and nuzzle him, ears forward to catch every caressing word.

Of course, O.J. rode and rode well. When he was not staying late in the school lab to work on some scientific project or other, he used to hang around the stables at Fairmont Farm, the big estate down the road. The grooms there were fond of him. He willingly cleaned out stalls, filled the water troughs, and curried the mares until their coats shone like polished bronze or well-waxed mahogany. In return for his help, the head groom, Mr. Lockhead, allowed him to exercise all but the most spirited stallion along the secluded bridle paths surrounding the parklike place.

Not even O.J.'s mother knew of this activity. The younger stableman had warned him that if the owner, Mrs. Bryan, found out that he frequented the estate, she would forbid him to come. O.J. imagined that this was the grooms' way of making sure that no one found out how much of their work a boy was doing, but he took no chances. His mother met Mrs. Bryan at bridge parties. She even helped sell tickets to the annual children's horse show sponsored by Mrs. Bryan. At thirteen, O.J. knew that neighbors gossip, and he knew that he was a loser.

School let out early in May. Captain Claymont was about to deliver microfiche mail and supplies to several outpost planets where earthmen had established U.S. Space Force guard stations and teams of scientists had set up bases for interstellar explorations. One morning

133

at breakfast the captain asked, "Now that school is out, would you like to come along, O.J.? Your mother agrees that you might enjoy the trip."

At first O.J. hesitated. What would the stablemen do without him? He ducked through the woods to the stables to confer with the head groom.

"Could you manage without me for a few months, Mr. Lockhead?" he asked. "You see, Dad has asked me to make the summer flight with him, and I guess he really needs my company."

Mr. Lockhead smiled. "Sure, lad, sure. We'll keep the horses in good shape until you get back. I'll even have a stall ready in case you bring back a colt of your own, so long as the critter's gentle and won't eat too many oats."

It was a long-standing joke—or was it a dream?— between them that someday O.J. would have a horse of his own, a small inconspicuous horse that he could stable with Mr. Lockhead. After all, who would know? Mrs. Bryan never came to the stables. When she did ride, the horses were brought around to the house. Besides, O.J. reasoned, a small beast wouldn't eat enough hay and oats to increase the feed bill much, and he could use his allowance to pay its expenses.

O.J. left with eyes as bright as stars in outer space.

The rocket ship was coming in for a landing. The auto-controls were set, the retro-rockets ready to fire. O.J. strapped himself into his reclining seat next to his father's. The automatic copilot was giving orders soundlessly through the microwave system to the robot crewmen whose mechanical brains figured wind velocity and speed and estimated the heat and gravity of the planet that seemingly rushed up to meet them.

"Dad," said O.J. through the intercom built into his

134

space suit, "it looks as if Hyperion is a planet with gravity just like Earth's." After seven previous landings, O.J. knew how to scan meters, dials, and gauges almost as well as his father.

"Not quite the same," replied Captain Claymont. "The G-meter shows a slightly greater pull of gravity here. You'll feel a bit heavy and sluggish when we disembark. Otherwise, you'll find conditions much like those of our planet. You won't need your helmet here."

The spacecraft's retro-rockets fired. The ship trembled. Then under two enormous fabrilon umbrellas, it settled gently to the ground. O.J. felt a jolt, heard the clank of landing gear against a boulder, saw the flashing signal lights, then experienced the roar of silence as the machinery whirred to a halt. He swallowed hard half a dozen times to adjust the pressure in his ears and unbuckled the restraint harness.

"Come, son. We'll leave through the cargo port as usual. I'll carry the registered microfiche mail to headquarters. Later, I'll come back with some of the boys to superintend the unloading of the supplies."

"Want me to guard the ship while you are gone?"

"That won't be necessary. There are only a few men here on space-patrol duty and no dangerous animals. In fact, the local creatures are so timid that Earth folk seldom even catch a glimpse of them. But look at the showy flowers."

O.J. carefully noted in his log: "Hyperion—spectacular flora; reticent fauna," tucked the notebook into the zippered pocket across his chest, straightened his space suit, and stepped off the loading platform at the end of the ship's pressure port. He landed with a surprising thud on the soft terrain, picked himself up, and started to walk to a grove of sequoialike trees half a kilometer away.

"Don't wander off too far," his father's voice warned over the telecom. "We'll be taking off in less than two hours—Earth time—and heading straight for home."

O.J. nodded, half turned, saluted, and pressed forward. The walking was not easy. He felt as if he were back on Earth, carrying a heavy pack on his shoulders or walking in the thick, dry sand of the dunes along the seashore.

When he reached a stand of mammoth trees, O.J. stopped to rest. That was when he first saw the beast. In an open glade, spotlighted by the rays of Hyperion's sun, the creature looked like a small golden statue of a horse with mane, tail, and hooves of silver. A horse—yet not quite like any horse O.J. had ever seen.

O.J. sucked in his breath. He froze where he stood, while the wild thing regarded him, head slightly turned on its arched neck, ears and tail erect. Almost in a whisper, O.J. started to talk.

"Come here, you beauty, you. Don't be afraid of me. I won't touch you if you don't want me to. But come just a little closer. Come."

With a shake of his magnificent mane and a throaty whinny, the creature moved forward, broke into a trot, and stopped abruptly two feet away from the excited boy.

"My name is O.J.," he murmured. "You are like an Earth horse—almost—except for those strange shoulders that look about ready to sprout wings. How I'd love to feel your coat, you beauty, you magnificent little stallion."

The two eyed each other for a full Earth minute. Then the horselike beast stepped forward and put his wet muzzle against the boy's cheek.

O.J. stroked the arched neck and the silvery mane and talked on and on in the quiet forest about how

136

much he wanted a horse of his own, about the kids who teased, and about his dream of someday winning a blue ribbon in a horse show. The beast made no reply, but O.J. knew he understood. Somehow, O.J. found he knew the creature's name. He felt a kind of silent communication that he could not explain. Pegasus—what an unusual name for a horse!

Suddenly, the quiet was shattered by the telecom. Captain Claymont was calling, telling him to return immediately to the rocket ship. After one last hug and a final word, O.J. turned away and started to plod back across the open space. There was a lump in his throat. He could not bear to look back.

Then he heard a bell-like whinny, glanced over his right shoulder, and found Pegasus walking lightly, silently, close behind him. With a joyous cry, he flung himself astride the animal, fingers grasping the light mane, knees gripping the silken flanks.

Captain Claymont stared as horse and rider mounted the port cargo lift. His son, with shining face, looked up at him and waved.

"Raise the elevator, Daddy," shouted O.J. "Pegasus wants to come with us, can't you tell? Pegasus is coming home with me!"

"We are not allowed to import exotic fauna," the captain called down to his son. "You know the Federal Space Patrol's Regulation 208 as well as I do."

"He's *not* exotic fauna; he's a horse, even if he does look a little different from Earth horses. I'll lead him off the ship at night. He'll pass for a palomino. We'll say we got him in Oregon. Daddy, please!"

Captain Claymont looked at O.J.'s flushed face. Poor kid, he thought, he's never been so happy in all his life.

Silently he raised the cargo lift, closed the hatch, and began to set the controls for a takeoff. As O.J. and the

137

creature entered the cabin, Captain Claymont said, "Fasten him to the side of the forward hold with two of the padded cargo belts. He'll be safer if you can get him to lie down on that pile of cargo protectors."

Pegasus immediately lay down, allowed himself to be blanketed in mats and secured by foot-wide, foam-padded belts that were attached to the walls of the rocket ship. Later, in outer space, he showed no fear of weightlessness, whereas a less intelligent creature might have been terrified. He floated effortlessly around the hold, drank water through a length of hose, and ate oats and hay from a tightly tied makeshift feed bag. O.J. was so busy caring for his new pet that the days passed quickly.

At last the trip was over. The rocket freighter was ferried to the mooring tower as a red Earth's sun sank into the fiery west. The ship's tender van rolled up to take off the return mail and the captain's personal possessions.

Captain Claymont plied the driver with interplanetary gossip and listened with more apparent interest than usual to the driver's tales of earthly wars and politics, while O.J. led a pad-covered Pegasus to the van. The sky was sprinkled with stars when the van slipped into the Claymonts' auto-port. The driver activated the forklift that gently scooped up and deposited on the astroturf the spaceman's belongings and, with them, a tired thirteen-year-old who stood protectively beside his blanketed treasure.

Before the sun was up, O.J. rode his strange stallion along the tree-lined bridle path that led to the stables of Fairmont Farm. Mr. Lockhead and his helper, already busy with their chores, looked up in surprise.

"So you found a critter after all," said Mr. Lockhead, studying Pegasus with a practiced eye. "An unearthly-looking beast if ever I saw one, but handsome in his way. He can't be more than twelve hands high and overly stocky in the shoulders. Still, his light chestnut coat's quite something, I must say—sets off that silvery mane and tail. I never saw his like before, and I've been around horses more than fifty years."

"He's a special sort of palomino," hedged O.J. "Gentle and smart." Entering the exercise ring, he put Pegasus through the proper paces of a pleasure horse—a walk, then a trot, then a canter. At last he pulled up before Mr. Lockhead and his assistant.

"Funny thing," said the assistant groom, after thoughtfully chewing on a straw, "he don't rightly seem to be cantering on the ground. I saw daylight under his hooves."

O.J. knew immediately what the trouble was. Earth's gravity was less than that of Hyperion, and Pegasus was designed for that other world. He could never explain *that* to the stablemen, so he rambled on to mask his concern.

"He's kind of light on his feet. Makes him a lovely pacer and fast at the gallop."

"Don't suppose you've heard that Mrs. Bryan's having her annual children's horse show next Friday?" said Mr. Lockhead. "Your beast might place in the Three-gaited Pleasure Horse Class, to be judged on manners and way-of-going. That little fellow does move well. Might even try for the Working Hunter Class, to be judged for soundness and performance at a fast canter. Can he jump?"

O.J. started to say, "I don't know," but before the words were out of his mouth, Pegasus trotted out into the ring where three fencelike jumps were set up. Holding some strands of the beautiful mane and gripping the smooth flanks with his knees, O.J. wondered how he could keep his seat without saddle or stirrups. He didn't have long to wonder.

Tensing the muscles beneath his gleaming coat, Pegasus broke into a gallop, rose into the air at least a foot above the first three-foot-high jump, and sank earthward as lightly as a feather carried in the wind. A few paces farther and he cleared the second jump, then the third. So effortless was his jumping and so delicate his recovery, that his young rider sat as steady as a statue of a general on his charger. Grinning, O.J. trotted up to the astonished grooms.

"Laddie, whoever taught you to sit to the jump like that?" Mr. Lockhead's voice was full of admiration.

"It was easy," O.J. said with a shrug. "You will keep him, the way you said you would, Mr. Lockhead? Won't you?"

"Yes, lad, I will. And I'll tell Mrs. Bryan you're entering the critter in the two other events and the Open Jumping Class as well. The programs go to the printer today. What did you say his name was?"

"Pegasus," said O.J. "By Rocket Ship out of Hyperion." He snickered at his private joke.

"Pegasus! Never heard tell of such a bloodline. What stable did you say he came from?"

O.J. said airily, "It's a Greek name. Some old Greek horse breeder. . . . He said the line came from the East somewhere . . . maybe Arabian. Well, I must be getting home. The school bus comes at eight."

After patting Pegasus on his velvet nose and thanking Mr. Lockhead for his help, O.J. took off along the bridle path, enormously pleased with himself. The assistant groom glowered angrily after O.J.'s retreating figure before leading Pegasus to the stall assigned to him.

The day of the horse show hung a gold October sun in a bright blue sky. O.J., who had been over to the stables every day to curry and exercise the wonder horse, arrived at Fairmont Farm well ahead of the other contenders. Mr. Lockhead had lent him a light saddle pad and fixed a bridle without a bit. O.J. had told his friend that Pegasus needed no bit because he understood his rider's thoughts and obeyed unspoken commands.

"Well," the old stableman had said, "use a bridle anyway, just for window dressing, like. And I'll fit him with a pad that'll all but hide those bumpy shoulder muscles. Never been done before, hereabouts, but I guess you can ride him without a saddle. Nothing in the rules against it that I know of. Sure you could jump without stirrups, in spite of the noisy crowd?"

"Of course," O.J. had replied. "You saw how easy it was."

"You sit him well, laddie. And the critter takes the jumps more like a bird than a horse. That mane and tail afloating in the breeze is as pretty a sight as these old eyes have ever seen. You might even win the blue ribbon in the Jumping Class."

O.J. watched the horse vans arrive. From each one descended eager young riders, proud parents, and sleek animals with shining coats of black, or chestnut, or dappled gray. Several schoolmates who lived nearby rode their mounts to the horse-show grounds and tethered them to hitching posts set up in the shade.

Soon cars arrived bearing spectators—mostly families and friends of the contestants—and parked with their headlights facing the ring. There was a babble of banter, punctuated by shouts of excited laughter and announcements over the loudspeaker.

O.J. stood alone near Pegasus' stall. Once he caught

141

a glimpse of a couple of his self-assured schoolmates swaggering about in well-cut britches and boots and wondered if he would make a fool of himself riding bareback into the ring in his jeans and sneakers. Then Pegasus whinnied softly and nuzzled his left ear until he felt that everything would be quite all right.

At three o'clock, Mrs. Bryan, Mr. Lockhead, and a man unfamiliar to O.J. took their places at the judges' table. On it were scoring pads for the judges' use and twelve gold-stamped ribbons—four blue, four red, and four yellow. In a place of honor in the center of the table stood a large two-handled silver cup, which sparkled in the sunlight. The high school band struck up "Stars and Stripes Forever," and the crowd grew quiet.

As the ringmaster entered the ring, an announcer spoke over the loudspeaker, "Good afternoon, ladies and gentlemen. Today's show will comprise four events. First, Junior Riders, aged eight to eleven, on Ponies and Small Pleasure Horses, to be judged for manners and way-of-going at a walk and trot. Second, Senior Riders, aged twelve to fourteen, on Three-gaited Pleasure Horses, to be judged on manners and way-of-going at a walk, a trot, and a canter. Next, there will be a Working Hunter Class for Senior Riders, horses to be judged at a walk, a trot, a canter, and a fast canter. The final event will be an Open Jumping Class, over jumps three feet high, to be judged for performance and manners. Scoring to be as follows: knocking down a rail to equal four points against performance; for first refusal to jump, three points; for two refusals to jump, six points. The first event is now called."

As the band played, the junior riders entered the show-ring in single file. O.J. rode up from the stables and joined the older riders outside the split-rail fence that formed the ring. Betsy, trim and smiling, called out to O.J., "Hello, there. I haven't seen you all summer. Where have you been?"

Before O.J. had a chance to answer, Jim Painter rode over to Betsy and quipped, "Which are you doing, Bets —smiling at the guy or laughing at his mount?"

Then, staring down from his fifteen-hand gelding, he said, "Hi, feller, are you and that animal on the program as contestants or as comic relief? We could all use a good laugh while the judges are scoring."

Several of the riders giggled. O.J. wanted to lash out at his tormentor . . . to fall through a hole in the turf . . . to cry like a kid. Red-faced, he sat staring at a distant hillside. Pegasus pawed the earth with a delicate hoof and tossed his fine head. Suddenly, O.J.'s anger and frustration vanished, and he was no longer tongue-tied.

"You can answer that question for yourself when the show's over," he said quietly before he rode away.

After the younger children had received their awards and left the ring, the band played another march. One by one, the senior contestants entered at a walk.

"Show your horses; show your horses," called the announcer.

The young riders, reminded, straightened their backs and tightened the reins. Pegasus, sensing what was expected, held his great head high and pranced like a circus horse. The judges made notes. Then the announcer called, "A slow trot; now a fast trot." A few moments later, he said, "Now canter."

Then the judging began. The contestants, quiet with anxiety, formed a line along the fence. A few horses, as nervous as their riders, refused to stand still and trotted back and forth out of control. Pegasus stood motionless, his head slightly turned, eyes on the judges. The

143

minutes ticked by at a snail's pace.

At length the ringmaster waved and the loudspeaker came alive. The announcer said, "Ladies and gentlemen, the winners of Class II, Senior Riders on Three-gaited Pleasure Horses, judged for manners and way-of-going, have been selected.

"The blue ribbon, for first place, goes to Pegasus, ridden by Otis J. Claymont, Jr. The red ribbon, for second place, is awarded to Merry-go-round, ridden by Miss Betsy Drake. And the gold ribbon, for third place, was won by Balliwick, ridden by Helen Walters."

The onlookers applauded as O.J., on Pegasus, the winner, circled the ring alone, at a fast trot. He smiled at his parents, who stood beaming beside their old 2009 Carrier Buggie parked near the exit gate. The other contestants followed him out, as was the custom.

The announcer next called the third event on the program.

"Ladies and gentlemen," he said, "I now call the Working Hunter Class for Senior Riders. Will all contestants in this division please enter the ring?"

Only seven of the older riders had the skill needed for this contest; for, in addition to walking, trotting, and cantering, each horse had to circle the ring at a fast canter or gallop. First in line was Jim Painter, on Crowned Head, his well-mannered thoroughbred. He gave a good account of himself, except that, halfway around the ring, the horse broke from a gallop into a trot.

Pegasus and O.J. were the second contestants. Small and unimpressive as they seemed in contrast to Jim on his tall gelding, nobody snickered. With the precision of a ballet dancer, the wonder horse carried his rider through the prescribed paces, and then stretched out in a breathtaking, almost airborne, gallop. Completing

144

the circle, he slowed to a fast trot and pranced out of the ring to thunderous applause.

With that exhibition of horsemanship, no other contestant could compete. It took the judges only a moment to make their decision. The blue ribbon was awarded to Pegasus. The red went to Crowned Head, whose owner received it sulkily. The gold was won by Dancing Lady, ridden by Carrie Dougherty.

Once again that day, O.J. circled the ring alone, riding like a conqueror—proud, sure, unmindful of the spectators who shouted and clapped as he passed. Once again, the other contestants followed him out of the ring. Then, just before she reached the exit gate, Betsy's filly lost a shoe. With tears in her eyes, Betsy dismounted and led her horse through the open gate.

"What's the matter, Betsy?" asked O.J. "Is something in your eye?"

"No," she said, swallowing hard. "Merry-go-round lost a shoe. I'll have to sit out the jumping. My last year, too—and I wanted so much to win a blue ribbon!"

Jim Painter smiled a crooked smile. "It's an ill wind that blows nobody any good, as they say. With you grounded, I'll take the blue for sure."

O.J. was furious at Jim's callousness. All the petty cruelty that he had suffered at the boy's hands ignited like a firecracker and burst in his brain. Pegasus pawed the grass and whinnied. O.J.'s anger disappeared. Startled, he received a message from the unearthly creature. The message, clear as a spoken word, recorded itself on his brain: "Let Betsy ride me in the jumping event. I promise that you will never regret it."

O.J. was sure that he had misunderstood. For days he had dreamed of riding Pegasus to victory. There must be some mistake.

145

Again Pegasus tossed his mane and whinnied lightly. Again the message came, this time with an added thought, "Hurry, there isn't much time. Tell her now."

Sighing, O.J. dismounted and walked over to Betsy. "Ride Pegasus in the jumps," he said. "You can still win if you ride Pegasus."

Betsy stared as if she had never seen O.J. before. "Are you being nasty, like Jim?" she asked.

"Of course not. Hurry up! They're calling the event." Betsy put the toe of her boot in O.J.'s cupped hands and mounted.

"Oh, my," she said. "He has no saddle and stirrups."

O.J. smiled fleetingly. "He has no bit either—that bridle's a phony. Just talk to him, and Pegasus will do anything you want. Go, go! They're closing the gate to the ring."

Betsy went, too flustered to say another word, and entered the ring at the end of the line. There were only five contestants.

The crowd quieted and held its breath as Jim on his big gelding moved forward, urged his mount into a canter, and took the first jump. Making the first half of a figure eight, the horse and rider turned at a trot, gathered speed, and cleared the second barrier. Turning again to complete the figure eight, Jim signaled his horse once more and headed at a fast gallop toward the third hurdle. The animal started to jump a fraction of a second too soon and came down short, dislodging the top bar of the third jump.

Although the next three riders made a creditable showing, none displayed outstanding horsemanship. Helen Walters, a bit younger than Betsy, was heartbroken when her horse refused one jump. Sam Eliott let his knees flap in the breeze so that when he jumped, everyone could see blue sky between his saddle and the seat of his breeches. Stauffer Gibbs won a round of applause for a good performance until it was discovered that he was too old to compete. He had passed his fifteenth birthday two days before the show and was disqualified.

Then it was Betsy's turn. Stirrupless, astride an unfamiliar horse, she found her courage slipping away, until she heard—or thought she heard, "Don't be afraid, Betsy. Sit tall, grasp my mane, and smile."

With that, the small creature trotted gaily forward, gathered speed like a tornado, and cleared the first jump by more than a foot. Landing featherlight, Pegasus wheeled. He flung himself over the second jump, turned at a fast gallop, and floated over the third. Finally, mane and tail streaming, he galloped from the ring with Betsy, flushed and happy, sitting proudly on his back. Only O.J., watching over the show-ring fence, noticed that the dainty, silvery hooves scarcely touched the ground. The crowd went wild.

While the three judges put their heads together, the band played another march. Then the announcer called, "Will the contestants in the Jumping Class please return to the ring and stand beside the bridles of their horses."

The five contestants rode in, formed a line down the center of the ring, and dismounted. O.J. wistfully hung back behind the fence, until Mr. Lockhead rose from the judges' table and waved him in.

As he trudged across the turf on foot, he passed Jim Painter who drawled, "What's the matter, Oh, 'tis Junior—lost your horse? It wasn't much to begin with, so it's a small loss." Too disconsolate to react to the taunt, O.J. found a place to the right of his little stallion.

The announcer asked for silence, then said, "Mrs. Bryan, sponsor of this annual event, will now hand out

147

the ribbons awarded by the judges."

Mrs. Bryan stepped into the ring, holding three ribbons, as the announcer reached for the judges' list handed to him by Mr. Lockhead.

"The winner of the Open Jumping Class, over jumps three feet high, is Pegasus, ridden by Miss Betsy Drake," said the announcer. With shining eyes, Betsy received the blue ribbon.

While the crowd applauded, Betsy looked across the velvet nose of the wonder horse and said, "O.J., this is the proudest moment of my whole life. I'll never forget you, never—you and Pegasus."

O.J. found himself actually smiling, and at a girl at that!

The red ribbon went to Crowned Head, Jim Painter's horse, whose scowling owner almost snatched it from Mrs. Bryan; while the gold was handed to Henry Summers, who was delighted to get a ribbon at all.

The band struck up the "Victory March" as Mrs. Bryan moved over to the judges' table and picked up the large, two-handled silver cup.

"And now, ladies and gentlemen," said the announcer importantly, "comes the high point of the show. Mrs. Bryan is about to award the silver cup to the contestant who, in the opinion of the judges, has shown not only fine horsemanship throughout this competition but also kindness and good sportsmanship. The winner of the Bryan Cup is Otis J. Claymont, Jr."

O.J., stunned, just stood beside Pegasus.

"Come forward, young man," said the ringmaster, and a velvet muzzle urged him on. The crowd roared. Band music drowned out the beating of O.J.'s heart.

O.J. held the cup carefully as he shook hands with Mrs. Bryan. She said, "Mr. Lockhead tells me that you handle horses well. I saw today that you are also generous and kind. Would you like a regular part-time job helping to exercise my horses?"

"Gee, thanks, Mrs. Bryan. Thanks a million." Clutching the precious cup, he walked back to Pegasus, mounted him, circled the ring, and headed back to the stables.

The crowds had streamed away and the horse vans were pulling out when Mr. Lockhead returned to bed down the animals at Fairmont Farm.

"Laddie," said the old man, "I'm right proud of you. That there critter performed like a circus horse—beautiful!"

O.J., who had been currying Pegasus, put his arms around the silken neck and said, "He's beautiful, all right, and smarter than any other horse alive."

Mr. Lockhead spoke carefully, picking his words like wild flowers. "Now I've got something to tell you. I decided it would keep until the show was over. That lazy, good-for-nothing stableboy I fired this morning reported your daddy to the Bureau for the Protection of Interplanetary Species. It's agin the law, as you know, to import critters from other planets. Your dad could get into a peck of trouble if the critter's not aboard his rocket freighter when he blasts off tomorrow on his autumn trip. His freight loader's coming right soon to truck the little fellow to the launchpad and put him aboard in a safety crate, right behind the pilot's cabin."

Mr. Lockhead studied O.J. for a while, then said, "You don't seem too surprised."

O.J. brushed the silvery mane with unusual care. Then he said, "Pegasus sort of told me . . . in the ring when he nuzzled me. Nothing so beautiful will ever happen to me again." A lump rose in O.J.'s throat, but the wonder beast whinnying, pawed the earth, and the lump dissolved.

"I guess we both knew he'd have to go back someday," said O.J., patting the shining flank. "Anyway, now the kids won't tease me anymore, and I have a real job with you here at the stables. I'll manage."

O.J. watched the setting sun transform the autumn leaves into flames of red, yellow, and gold. Deep inside, he knew that from now on his world would be a better place to live in.

Other Worlds, Other Times
—Books You Will Enjoy

Alexander, Lloyd. *The Book of Three.* Holt, Rinehart & Winston, Inc., 1964.

———. *Time Cat.* Holt, Rinehart & Winston, Inc., 1963.

Asimov, Isaac. *I, Robot.* Doubleday & Company, Inc., 1950.

Christopher, John. *The White Mountains.* The Macmillan Company, 1967.

de Camp, L. Sprague, and Catherine C. (eds.). *Tales Beyond Time.* Lothrop, Lee & Shepard Co., Inc., 1973.

———. *3,000 Years of Fantasy and Science Fiction.* Lothrop, Lee & Shepard Co., Inc., 1972.

del Rey, Lester. *The Runaway Robot.* The Westminster Press, 1965.

———. *Tunnel Through Time.* The Westminster Press, 1966.

Engdahl, Sylvia L. *Enchantress from the Stars.* Atheneum Publishers, 1970.

———. *This Star Shall Abide.* Atheneum Publishers, 1972.

Heinlein, Robert A. *Have Space Suit—Will Travel.* Charles Scribner's Sons, 1958.

———. *Podkayne of Mars.* G. P. Putnam's Sons, 1963.

———. *Star Beast.* Charles Scribner's Sons, 1954.

Jakes, John. *Time Gate.* The Westminster Press, 1972.

Key, Alexander. *Escape to Witch Mountain.* The Westminster Press, 1968.

——. *The Forgotten Door.* The Westminster Press, 1965

Le Guin, Ursula. *A Wizard of Earthsea.* Parnassus Press 1968.

L'Engle, Madeleine. *A Wrinkle in Time.* Farrar, Straus & Company, Inc., 1962.

Lewis, C. S. *The Lion, the Witch and the Wardrobe.* The Macmillan Company, 1951.

Norton, André. *Star Gate.* Harcourt, Brace and Company, Inc., 1958.

O'Brien, Robert C. *Mrs. Frisby and the Rats of Nimh* Atheneum Publishers, 1971.

Tolkien, J. R. R. *The Hobbit.* Houghton Mifflin Company, 1938.

White, Ted. *Secret of the Marauder Satellite.* The Westminster Press, 1967.